A Fine and Private Place

A Fine and Private Place

ELLERY QUEEN

G.K. Hall & Co. • Chivers Press
Waterville, Maine USA Bath, England

This Large Print edition is published by G.K. Hall & Co., USA and by Chivers Press, England.

Published in 2002 in the U.S. by arrangement with The Frederic Dannay Literary Property Trust, The Manfred B. Lee Family Literary Property Trust and their agent, JackTime of 3 Erold Court, Allendale, NJ 07401, USA.

Published in 2002 in the U.K. by arrangement with the Frederic Dannay Literary Property Trust and the Manfred B. Lee Family Literary Property Trust.

U.S. Softcover   0-7838-9759-6   (Paperback Series Edition)
U.K. Hardcover   0-7540-4794-6   (Chivers Large Print)
U.K. Softcover   0-7540-4795-4   (Camden Large Print)

The text of this Large Print edition is unabridged.
Other aspects of the book may vary from the original edition.

Set in 16 pt. Plantin.

Printed in the United States on permanent paper.

British Library Cataloguing in Publication Data available

Library of Congress Cataloging-in-Publication Data

Queen, Ellery.
   A fine and private place / Ellery Queen.
     p. cm.
   ISBN 0-7838-9759-6 (lg. print : sc : alk. paper)
   1. Police — New York (State) — New York — Fiction. 2. Fathers and sons — Fiction. 3. New York (N.Y.) — Fiction. 4. Novelists — Fiction. 5. Large type books. I. Title.
PS3533.U4 F55 2002
813′.52—dc21
                                    2001051694

LT-M

"The grave's a fine and private place."
— ANDREW MARVELL,
TO HIS COY MISTRESS

"So is the womb."
— GEORGE WHALLEY,
POETIC PROCESS

Contents

PRECONCEPTION

Under normal conditions the ovum lies in the uterus for about 24 hours. Waiting.

August 9, 1962

Wallace Ryerson Whyte stepped out into space with an astronaut's confidence that the laws of the universe would not let him fall. Faith sustained him: he remained suspended over the East River, hidden far below by the mists that had gathered after the soaking day at the dropping temperatures of twilight.

The narrow little penthouse balcony with its guardian stone gargoyles had been a conceit of its *fin de siècle* architect, venting his homosexual dislike for the giddy ladies of his era. The tall man never gave it a thought. He leaned on the parapet and settled himself to use what time he had.

He was puffing characteristically on a $250 Charatan pipe loaded with Medal of Honor tobacco at a dollar an ounce, and characteristically there was an ember burn on the brown velvet lapel of his Edwardian jacket. The ember was still daintily glowing. But he was trying to penetrate the murk stirring below to the reason for Importuna's summons and he did not notice the burn. He concentrated with his rather oriental eyes. They were squinty outdoors eyes deliberately trained to go with the saddle-leather of his face, which had been weathered in his

9

club. He was tall and contained, his elegance a touch raffish; not quite the man of distinction. He contrived to conceal his intelligence behind the façade of his lineage, which was overgrown with the dusty virtues of his class. His father had long ago disinherited him, making him the first male of his line in three generations to have to work for a living.

He puffed and mused.

It was a serious matter, obviously. He had had occasion to visit one or another of the three uppermost apartments at Number 99 East often enough, for private accountings or other confidential business connected with the Importuna Industries conglomerate, but Nino Importuna did not invite his executives to his penthouse after office hours for ordinary business. Or ordinary pleasure, either.

A small tremolo fluttered the smoker's spine.

Nino had found out.

God had found out.

Judgment Day . . .

The tall man was tapping his pipe on the parapet, watching the sparks die away and reflecting on his options, when a nasty voice said from the drawing room, "Sir?" making the syllable sound as if it were composed of four letters. He turned with reflexively inquiring brows, covering up by habit. It was Nino's muttonchopped man, Crump, who had admitted him to the penthouse. Crump was one of the few hallmarked English butlers left on Manhattan Island, and he possessed the sixth sense of his breed. "Mr. Importuna will see you now. Sir. If you will follow me?"

He sauntered after the man, trying to ignore the spiteful flunky back, thinking how much better the mural ceiling, the pastry arabesque-work of the walls, the grand marble fireplace, the quatrefoiled cathedral windows suited him than Importuna. But the thought was like the tobacco sparks. True, he had never entirely accommodated himself to the central fact of his existence, which was that he had no talent for making the Importuna kind of money — how many men had? — but he did not allow this failing to hobble his life style. Above all he was a practitioner of the possible.

Crump glided before him to the threshold of the holy of holies, stepped aside, and — between successive blinks, he could have sworn — departed through a solid wall.

In the sanctum, behind a pontifical Florentine table that had descended authentically from a Medici, sat its pontiff. Nino Importuna was a squat man whose broad and fleshy body had been built by the genes of peasants and a child-hood of pasta — corporally a very ordinary-looking southern Italian type. But his massive head was far from ordinary. The nose jutted from his face like a bowsprit. The small mouth seemed womanishly soft, but this was a decep-tion of nature: when he smiled and exhibited his very large white teeth, which was seldom, the softness turned into something terrifying. There was an olive-oil patina to the darkness of his barbered cheeks and jowls that toned well with the dull gloss of his black-dyed hair. But it was the eyes underneath the strong, still naturally black brows that gave his face its commanding character. The color of stale, muddy espresso, they were bitter and without warmth or love, almost without humanity . . . the eyes of an enemy.

These eyes were fixed on the tall man. Their owner's hands were pressed together in the Dürer attitude, at his chin; lids half shut. But the industrial genius of the Importuna empire was not praying; and to the visitor the eyes were not half shut but half open — not drooping from fatigue but on the slitted qui vive.

It was bad, all right.

"*Entrate pure.*" There was as usual nothing to be interpreted from the heavy Italian-American voice. Or perhaps it had been just a few decibels more resonant? He waved toward a chair.

The tall man came obediently in and sat down. The chair was dumpy, like Importuna, with protuberant carving in bumps and lumps that made sitting almost intentionally uncomfortable. Yes, very bad. . . . Nino called this room, with semantic fidelity, his den. A den it was, windowless and dim, and foul with the stench of his crooked-stogy smoke, his $10-an-ounce aftershave, and whatever it was he rubbed into his coarse gray hair to blacken it; the only smell missing was of stale blood, from old kills.

The tall man smiled at his fancy.

"You're happy today?" Importuna said.

"Beg pardon?"

"You're smiling. Did you just enjoy a woman?"

"Hardly, Nino. I came directly here from the office when I got your message."

"Then what are you smiling at?"

The famous Importuna technique.

"Nothing, Nino." The famous employee defense. "Just something that passed through my mind."

"A joke question?"

"No. Well, yes. In a way."

"What? Tell me, *amico*. Today I would like to hear something to make me smile, too."

The tall man found his shoes burrowing into the silk pile of the Kashan rug, which dated from the early 17th century and Shah Abbas and should have been hung reverently on a wall; he stopped shuffling with a feeling of desecration. He was no longer smiling; in fact, he was becoming angry. This would never do. Not with Nino. You had to match Nino's cool.

He made an effort and composed himself.

"It's nothing, really," he repeated. "Let's get on with it, Nino, shall we? Whatever it is. Whatever's on your mind." A mistake, he thought with a sinking feeling. It showed fear. You never showed fear to Nino, because then he had you.

"You don't know?"

"No, Nino, I don't."

13

This time it was Importuna who smiled. What big teeth you have, Grandpa.

"Superba Foods?" Importuna said suddenly. "L.M.T. Electronics? Harris-Fuller Farm Implements? Ultima Mining?"

"Yes?" The tall man was really proud of himself; his eyes had not so much as flickered. Even his breathing remained under control. "What about them, Nino?"

"Now you're being coy with me," Importuna said. "Or *stupido*. And you are not *stupido*; I don't employ controllers who are *stupido*. So my vice-president the controller is playing the game of innocence. To play the game of innocence is to admit your guilt. *Bene?*"

"I wish I knew what you were talking about, Nino."

"Guilt," Importuna repeated through the oversized teeth. The smile added stress to the word, like a written underlining. It tied little knots in the tall man's back. But he maintained his puzzled posture.

He shook his head carefully. "Guilt, Nino? Guilt about what?"

"L.M.T. Ultima. Superba. Harris-Fuller."

"I heard you the first time. I still don't understand."

"They're companies owned by the conglomerate?"

"Of course."

"You're controller in those companies?"

"What's the point, Nino?"

"You are *stupido* after all." Importuna gripped a fresh stogy in his teeth and leaned back in his tall swivel chair. "But then to think you could get away with your beautiful false bookkeeping without my finding out, Mr. Controller Vice-President Big Shot High Liver Whoremaster Gambler, is all by itself the sign of a fool. Not that you haven't been smart the way you manipulated the figures. You're a real magician with figures; I always said it. It looked too easy to you, hey? A little here, a little there, some from this company debited to that and from that company posted to a third — you thought you could pull this stuff for years under my nose. Maybe it was luck, *amico* — your bad luck, my good luck — that I found out at all?" He lit the stogy and, like a one-man firing squad, directed a burst of acrid smoke across the great table. "What do you think?"

"Oh, I agree," the tall man said. "A man would have to be a fool, Nino, as you say. He'd never have a Chinaman's chance against you."

The large head wagged.

"Now you insult me. You're still playing games. You think I'm guessing, trying to trap you when I don't really have the goods on you? Another of your mistakes, *amico*. I sent an expert to examine your books. Under cover, of course."

The controller said slowly, "That new man, Hartz."

"*S'intende*. He reports to me that my smart controller–vice-president has stolen from me

15

and my brothers over the past three years over $300,000. What's more, he brought me the proofs. If I turn the proofs over to the district attorney and the Internal Revenue, Mr. Controller, you'll spend what is left of your life either in Sing Sing or the Danbury prison, depending on whether New York State or the federal government gets its hands on you first. You were going to say?"

"You might offer the condemned man a cigar."

Importuna looked surprised. He extended the box of stogies.

"Not those, if you don't mind," the tall man said. "The Havanas you keep for your peers are more to my taste."

"Your taste," the tycoon said, smiling for the third time. "Oh, yes." He picked up the antique Florentine dagger he used as a letter opener, and with it he nudged a tooled-leather humidor toward the other side of the table. The controller opened it, scooped out a handful of big fat fragrant green cigars, lit one, slipped the others carefully into his breast pocket, sat back, and puffed with enjoyment.

"I don't know what you paid the man who smuggled these in from Cuba for you, Nino, but they'd be a bargain at triple the price. How can you keep polluting the atmosphere with those ghastly black pretzels of yours when you've got these to smoke? But what I was about to say, Nino," he went on, "is that if you've called me up here this evening to talk about it, you've something other than policemen and income tax people in mind for me. That was clear from the start. Of course, I couldn't be altogether sure. I mean, if I seemed a bit nervous, I'll admit I was. But now I'm positive. Your so-called proofs are the lever with which you're trying to shove me into a deal. You want something for your money, and I've apparently got it."

"That," Importuna said with the soft smile, his fourth, "is not the saying of the *stupido* I took you for."

"I feel fairly safe in assuming that, with your usual efficiency and thoroughness, you've gone into my activities in depth. So you probably know where the allegedly borrowed funds went, and how, and you know as well that I haven't a dime of it left — that I'm additionally in debt, in fact, way over my head. So you can't be expecting restitution. At least not in kind. So what's the quid pro quo, Nino? What do I have that you could possibly want?"

"Virginia."

For a moment the tall man sat quite still. As he sat his eyes darkened to a deep sea blue. "Virginia," he said, as if it were a word he had never heard before.

"Virginia," the industrialist repeated, tasting it.

He took the Havana out of his mouth, peering at its smoke. "Well, I don't know, Nino. This isn't your mountainside Italy. Or the 19th cen-

17

tury. By the way, you are proposing to marry my daughter, aren't you? Not just play some dirty bedroom game with her?"

"Maiale! E figlio d'un maiale!"

The tall man sat unmoved by the almost visible steam coming out of the espresso eyes. He was a little surprised at Importuna's wrath; the old cod must really like the girl. The man behind the table sank back, fuming. "Yes, she's to be my wife," he said curtly. "Don't make me mad again. What I say to you is this: You talk Virginia into marrying me, and I not only won't prosecute you for embezzling Importuna money, I'll even pay your debts — $46,000, isn't it?"

"Forty-eight and some," the embezzler said delicately.

"— because then, you see, you'll be my father-in-law. My *suocero,* as they say in the old country. Family. You know how we take care of family . . . *suocero.*"

"I'm a bit young for the role," the controller murmured, "but unsuccessful thieves are like beggars, Nino, aren't they?" He stuck the cigar back between his teeth. "At that I'm not sure I understand. You say you want to marry Virginia. You've never struck me as an Italian Miles Standish. You usually speak right up when you want something. How come you haven't asked her? Or have you?"

"Many times."

"Then she's turned you down."

"Each time . . ." Importuna was about to say

more. Instead, he crushed his stogy out.

"Then how do you expect me to get her to change her mind? You've been an American long enough to know that dutiful daughters and arranged marriages went out with bundling and the bustle."

"You'll find an argument, *suocero*. For instance, you might mention to her certain funds you took that didn't belong to you? The hardness of the mattresses in Sing Sing and Danbury? The disgrace of your old family name? I leave the approach to you, *amico*. In view of your fate otherwise, I have confidence you won't fail."

"You talk like a damned soap opera, you know that?" the embezzler muttered; most of his mind was already occupied with tactics. "Look, Nino, it isn't going to be that easy. Virginia has a mind of her own —"

"But she loves you," Importuna said. "Though the good Jesus alone knows why."

"And that's another thing. There's the religious difference —"

"She will convert to the Church. That's to be understood."

"Just like that? Suppose she simply won't go along, Nino. There's no guarantee even with the prison argument."

"That's your problem. Always remembering," Importuna said, "that if you don't deliver I charge you with grand larceny."

The Havana went out. He took it out of his

mouth, regarded it with regret, and set it down on Importuna's ashtray. "How much time are you giving me?"

"Ah," the swarthy man said briskly. "Today is August 9th. I'm allowing you one month to talk her into it. One month to the day. I want to marry Virginia on the 9th of September."

"I see." He was silent. Then some residue of decency made him say, "You know, Nino, rogue and peasant slave though I am, Virginia's my little girl still, and to think of playing on her feelings for me to force her into the arms of a man three times her age —"

"Shall I cry, *amico?*" Importuna said. "You're beginning to bore me. You'd sell her to an Arab if you could and there were enough money in it. Yes, I was born on September 9th, 1899, so I'll be 63 next month, and Virginia is 21, making me exactly three times her age, as you say. It would be a perfect day for a marriage; the numbers are very good, *perfetto.*"

"But three times . . ."

"I said no more!" Importuna shouted.

The tall man was startled. "All right, Nino," he said, "all right."

Importuna subsided, muttering in Italian. Finally he looked up. "Don't stand in the way of this. I want her. You understand? You can point out to her what she gets by marrying me. I give my promise, on my mother's memory, that she will have anything and everything she asks for. I offer her villas, chateaux, palaces — you know

20

my properties. A private yacht, one of the biggest; bigger than Onassis's, than Niarchos's. A jet of her own. Jewels — by the pound, if she likes. Clothes designed just for her by any or all of the great designers. Anything. Everything."

"Everything but a young husband in her bed," the tall man said. He did not quite know why he said it. He regretted the taunt immediately. A kind of boiling began to take place in the depths of the coffee-colored eyes. But then the hands, which had tightened about the dagger, relaxed and went Dürer again.

"Is that so much to give up," Importuna asked icily, "when she gets so much? Spare me the fatherly sentiment, *amico*. I know you for what you are."

Maybe you do and maybe you don't, the tall man said silently. Aloud he said, "Then that's the deal?" When Importuna shook his head the tall man said, "There's more to it, of course."

"*Sì davvero, caro mio.* There will be a before-marriage paper — an agreement which Virginia will sign."

"What kind of agreement?"

"It will say that she consents to have no property claim against me or my estate, not even the ordinary dower right, for five whole years after the wedding. This is so that she will not become my wife and then leave me. But if she sticks to our bargain — if she's still my wife and living with me on September 9th, 1967 — then she becomes my heir. My only heir, *suocero*. How does that grab you, as they say? Could anything be fairer than that?"

"There's the little matter of good faith between man and wife," the prospective father-in-law began; then he stopped and laughed. "No, you certainly have the right to protect yourself under the, uh, circumstances." He reached over, retrieved the Havana, and relit it. "But, Nino . . ."

"Ora che cos'è?"

"On September 9, 1967 you'll be — let's see — 68? Since we're speaking frankly," he said through a dribble of Cuban smoke, "I have to raise the disagreeable possibility that you may no longer be with us on that date. What happens to my daughter if you should die before the expiration of the agreement? She'd be left holding a very empty bag."

"Yes," Importuna said, "and so would you."

"But, Nino, that could mean she'll have wasted up to as much as five years of her young life. That doesn't seem right —"

"I agree, *amico*. But it's a chance she'll have to take. Is it such a bad gamble? Considering the stakes? Besides, try to see it from my point of view."

"Oh, I do, Nino. Still, Virginia's all I have. Her mother is dead, as you know. Not a single relative we know of left on either side —"

"My poor future *suocero*. I bleed with you. But what do they say? You won't be losing a daughter, you'll be winning a son-in-law."

"So true," the tall man murmured. "Well, Nino, I can only say I'll do my damnedest. Oh, yes. About those proofs . . ."

"What about them?"

"Nothing, nothing."

"I keep my bargains," Importuna said. "Do you doubt my word?"

"Certainly not —"

"And you may keep your controllership and the vice-presidency. You pull this off and I may even raise your salary, give you stock. But I warn you, Mr. Big Shot."

"About what, Nino?"

"No more borrowings from Superba Foods, Ultima Mining, the others. Little borrowings that add up so fast to so much. *Capito?*"

"Of course. Naturally."

"And no more magic tricks with the books. Hartz will be checking you."

"Nino, I give you my word —"

"And don't offer Hartz a cut of your thievings to give me false reports — there will be someone you don't know double-checking *him*. Not that I give nine damns in hell whether you rot in jail or not, *caro*. But how would it look for the wife of Nino Importuna? Her own father. Excuse me." He picked up one of the battery of telephones on the Florentine table, the one that was discreetly buzzing. "Yes, Peter."

"Mr. E just got in from Australia," a man's voice said.

23

"Mr. E? He's here? In the apartment?"

"Waiting."

"Good, Peter! I want to see him right away."

Importuna hung up and waved his right hand to his visitor in dismissal. He appeared no more self-conscious about the hand in waving it a few feet from the tall man than when he had kept it in sight on his chin during their long conversation. The hand possessed only four fingers; where the index and middle fingers should have been there was a single finger of double thickness, a sort of digital Siamese twin.

It was curiously flexible.

"Ciao, suocero," the nine-fingered multimillionaire said gently.

CONCEPTION

Under normal conditions the ovum lies in the uterus for about 24 hours, waiting.

If fertilization takes place, then, instead of passing through the uterus into the world of waste, the organism — now a zygote — attaches itself to the uterus wall and sets about its built-in program of growth.

From the Diary of
Virginia Whyte Importuna

December 9, 1966

I wonder why I keep adding to this, oh, *construction*. This higgledy-piggledy, slam-bang architecture of feelings . . . hopes, disappointments, terrors, joys, the lot. Is it because of the joys? The few I have? And the almost addictive need to express them? Then why do I keep dwelling on the bad scenes? Sometimes I think this isn't worth the risk. If N. were ever to find you, Diary . . . Well, what could he do? After all!

Plenty.

He would, too. And not just to daddy.

Let's face it, Virginia. He's got you by the lady parts.

I feel . . . Today was the Bitch of Time. A bad one, yea, verily. It began on that marvelous self-generating morning note of hope, rising, raising the flesh really in a gorgeous thrill of beauty digging deep and a sense of much more under *that*, like Sutherland at the Met when she's in top voice . . . Oh, stop drooling along like some

27

ninny teen-ager rolling around in her first crush. At the age of twenty-five! And allegedly married.

The fact is I was on the upsurge, wanting, wanting to be alone with P., not daring even to *look* at him with that monstrous kipper of a Crump around watching with those fried eyes of his while that prissy mouth shapes those luscious "Madams" that sound as if he's tasting me.

And old Editta with her red and squishy nose. I swear it twitched this morning when P. and I happened to nearly collide in the hall outside my dressing room. Or is that the hem of my guilt showing? To be afraid of a personal maid who can hardly utter an intelligible sentence in her own language, let alone mine!

I'm growing paranoid. The old soul's probably coming down with the flu and wishing I'd bathe and undress myself for bed once. Editta *cara,* I wish I could. Why N. insists on this slavish servitude, as if I were a sultana, I'm not quite sure. Of course, he's the sultan, so I suppose it's a matter of *his* image, *his* ego, not mine. I exist for greeting and planning and hostessing and being decorative around his kowtowing friends and underlings and big-belly business associates from Europe, North Africa, the Middle East — a kind of glorified five-star housekeeper, as P. truly calls me (but not in N.'s hearing!).

There, I've got rid of the poor thing for tonight, anyway. I had to reassure her that the *signore* would never, never know. Maybe we could work out an accommodation, Editta and I, for the future. Happy, wishful thought. She's so dad-blamed, all-fired scared of Nino, all he has to do is give her one of those evil-eye looks of his and she wets her *mutandine,* as Julio says with his customary refinement. And not from passion, either, she's past the age. Poor Editta.

Poor me. A bitch of a day, I repeat. My "cover," as the spy boys call it (don't they? or am I misusing the term? I must consult P., he knows everything) — anyway, my cover, or cover-up, or excuse, or alibi, or whatever, was that I was to do some Christmas shopping (Saks, Bergdorf's, Bonwit's, Georg Jensen, Mark Cross, Sulka, Brentano's — the circuit), which would put me out of range of Crump's Halloween eyes and Editta's bunny nose and into the blessed pollution of Fifth Avenue, the tintinnabulation of the Santa bells, and the trivial perils of purse snatchers, panhandlers, and muggers. And with N. skillions of miles away, in West Berlin or Belgrade or Athens or wherever, scheming how to make his millions propagate more millions — what did Julio, or was it Marco, say yesterday the conglomerate is now worth, cold turkey? close to *half a billion dollars?* how does anyone digest sums like that! — with *him* on the other side of an ocean I was *free* . . . free to spend most of the day with Peter! Even to be reckless. Such as now, writing his name full out and fancied up like H*y*m*a*n K*a*p*l*a*n's . . .

P*E*T*E*R.

P*E*T*E*R E*N*N*I*S.

There! Oh, Peter darling . . .

We were reckless sure enough. Luckily no harm was done. I think. But the way it turned out . . . Peter's denouement . . . I don't know. Who knows where harm lies? From which direction it can come, and when, and even why? Am I being paranoid really? Peter says that life in New York these days is an unending game of Russian roulette to which one either becomes inured or goes crackers. And after a while one even challenges it, he says — dares it sassily to do its lethal worst. While all the time, under the bravado, there cowers the wee sleekit mousie of a person being just — plain — damned — scared.

What's a mugger in the dark behind you with a knife blade at your throat compared with being in the clutches of a demon like N.?

Dreadful thought. I've waked up well over a thousand times saying thank God it was a nightmare and finding out it wasn't.

I know people would consider me off my bloody wicket if they could hear me sound off about N. like this. Why, darling, he's the kindest, most generous — and richest — man on four continents! And he absolutely, positively adores you, loves you *madly*. Oh, N. loves me madly, all right, the way a Jivaro loves his favorite shrunken head. Love . . . They should know what that word means to him. And what it means for a girl to have to endure over four years of . . .

I need a drink, dear Diary.

Better.

It's getting late and I've made hardly a start chronicling the day's events. Well, who gives a flying damn? Excuse me again, Diary. That tasted like more.

Everything a wife could ask for. Their envy tells me *that*. Oh, yeah? I'd like to see the wife.

May as well set the bottle handy. Handy brandy. Can't think of a rhyme for "cognac." Except "Zatzo, Mac?" and that wouldn't take fourth prize in a contest for idiots.

I wonder if Savonarola looked anything like Nino. One of these days I must look up a portrait of the kindly old far of Ferrari. I'll bet their profiles match.

What Nino really looks like is a wicked, wicked version of Federico Fellini, that's what. I'm chained to an aging Fellini image who creates whole planets of illusion with a wave of his fat, wet hands. Those nine fingers of his . . . They *revulse* me.

It's unkind of me. Really unfeeling. Nino can't help an accident of birth any more than the Minotaur and Quasimodo could help theirs. I wouldn't shrink from a man with, say, a gross harelip (unless he tried to kiss me, ugh). But something about that rubbery two-ply digit of his gives my stomach elevator-dropitis. And when he touches me with it . . . or should I say them? . . .

And his ridiculous superstitions. Beyond

31

belief. Imagine a leading power in the business world, an authentic big wheel, one of the grand moguls of Wall Street, the Bourse, and points east, actually dropping the last two letters of his surname, the name of his father and grandfather and great-grandfather, and having the poor circumcised thing (that's a bad metaphor, considering its location) conferred on him by the official act of a judge just because the name he was born with didn't conform to his lucky number! That's what's called bending fate to your will with a vengeance. He really believes in that nonsense. Not even Marco, who was born to be the prophet's disciple, can swallow that, though he does a manful little job of trying. This name business is about the only thing I can sometimes like Marco and Julio for. Editta's told me what pressure Nino — Big Brother — used on them to get them to drop the final *t-o* of Importunato the way he did. But they never would.

What I seem to have tonight is writer's wanderlust. Is what I seem to have tonight. No tittle, jot, or iota of discipline. Look who was going to be the Emily Dickinson of the 20th century! Only, how can the Muse compete with a third of half a billion dollars? Not to mention loyalty to a daddy who can't keep his hands off other people's property, thereby getting me into this hell of a hole in the first place? Oh, dad, dear dad, if only I didn't love you, damn you, I'd let you rot where you belong, which is up the river and under the trees — six feet under. And you'd take your leave with your O so charming smile, and butterfly kiss on the back of my neck . . . the kind you used to plant there when I was very small in the chest and very large in the jealous-of-mama department, whose face I can't even remember any more.

I was browsing through Blake's "Songs of Experience" after dinner hunting up old friends, when "A Poison Tree" renewed our acquaintance:

> *I was angry with my friend:*
> *I told my wrath, my wrath did end.*
> *I was angry with my foe:*
> *I told it not, my wrath did grow.*
>
> *And I water'd it in fears*
> *Night and morning with my tears,*
> *And I sunned it with smiles,*
> *And with soft deceitful wiles.*
>
> *And it grew both day and night,*
> *Till it bore an apple bright,*
> *And my foe beheld it shine,*
> *And he knew that it was mine,*
>
> *And into my garden stole*
> *When the night had veil'd the pole;*
> *In the morning, glad, I see*
> *My foe outstretch'd beneath the tree.*

I hadn't read it in years. It's rather awful, I

think, although once I doted on it. But it does about sum me up just now, I mean what's been going on away down inside where the heat's unbearable. The San Virginia Fault. Guaranteed to give anybody's seismograph the hotfoot when least expected.

Anyway.

Peter and I had an argument ("I was angry with my friend") about where to meet. For some reason it seemed terribly vital to both of us. He was in as hard a case as I was, but oppositely oriented. He was in his Goddam Nino Mood, during which he usually threatens to shove Nino's teeth down his throat. This time he wanted to climb up on the 43rd Street marquee of the Biltmore with a bullhorn, where everyone coming out of Grand Central on Vanderbilt and walking along Madison in the other direction could hear him proclaim our star-crossed love — everyone, including any passing newspaper reporter. I mean he actually opted for Le Pavilion, or 21, or that impossible restaurant everybody's flocking to where the maître d' insults you or refuses to seat you no matter who you are, in fact the better known you are the nastier he can get, and I said positively no, Peter, in those omnium-gatherums it's all grapevine, the word would reach Nino in two hours in Addis Ababa, if that's where he is; and Peter said, "So what? The sooner the better!" He was being absolutely suicidal.

In the end we compromised on my choice,

which was a dowdyish, unfashionable hideaway daddy had once taken me to (if they're hidden away, old daddums knows 'em!), where there was no chance anybody we or Nino knew would spot us. And the food's better than in a lot of the toity places where they even charge your date for the look the cigaret girl allows him down her cleavage.

Somehow, being out in public with Peter for the first time, which I'd thought was going to be a supergas, turned out to depress me wonderfully. I certainly wasn't at my best. For one thing, I don't know why I picked the Pozzuoli A-line to wear, I loathe it, it makes me look as if I were hiding a pregnancy in a muumuu, which I loathe also; they're great only if you're in the ninth month or have the hips of Babar. And the coat I wore over it, the cashmere with the queen-sized Russian lynx collar, which I'd selected from the mixed herd in my closet because it's the least conspicuous winter coat my lavish husband has allowed me to buy, had a hideous stain of some sort right in front, which I hadn't noticed and which I couldn't hide without laying back the coat, thus revealing the hated A-line. It was a total disaster.

In the second place, I was jolly-jelly-legged with funk in fear of being seen in spite of our precautions.

And thirdly, instead of acting the wise and understanding male and sticking to brilliantly innocuous table talk, Peter insisted on pounding away at me again about divorcing Nino and marrying him. As if I didn't want to!

"Peter, what's the point of going into that again?" I said in my most reasonable tone of voice. "You know it's impossible. I'd like some glogg, please."

"In this Greasy Spoon you picked?" Peter said, giving me his most hateful smile. "They wouldn't know what you're talking about, dear heart. My suggestion is to order beer. That they'll understand. And nothing's impossible. There has to be a way."

"I'm cold, I want something hot," I said. "And sarcasm isn't your strong point. I repeat, impossible. I can't leave Nino, Peter. He won't let me."

"How about an ordinary prole-type Tom and Jerry? There's a fighting chance they'll know what that is. How do we know he won't give you a divorce unless you ask him?"

"Peter, no! Because you're so close to him all day doesn't mean you know him. I tell you there's no chance he'd let me go, none at all, even aside from the religious reason. Oh, I'm sorry we were so foolish today. I have a feeling we're going to regret going out together like this."

"He really has you petrified, hasn't he? Well, he doesn't petrify me!"

"I know, dear, you're old lion guts, while I'm the original chicken. Besides, there's daddy to consider."

Peter's really sexy mouth drooped. Daddy is a subject we try not to kick around. Peter knows how I feel, and he does what he can to respect my feelings, but he never makes a very good job of it. Peter's trained himself to be the unobtrusive backgrounder, like Winstons and confidential secretaries should, but he's just too beautifully tall and broad and dark-gold-blond and God-bless-American good-looking and gray-blue-green-eyed (depending on what's going on in his glands at the moment) to get by unnoticed all the time; I mean I at least can read him like a traffic signal. There was a big red light coming up.

So I suppose in trying to avoid it I stepped on the gas too hard and blabbed what I'd never told anyone, especially Peter. And did it the worst way — jokingly, as if it were some belly buster, the yuk of yuks.

"Oh, let's stop talking about daddy," I said cutely. "Do you know I have a pet name for my husband?"

Peter reacted as if I'd shot him. "A *pet* name? For *Nino?*"

"Sickening, isn't it?"

"You've got to be kidding. I mean, you are, aren't you?"

"Not a bit of it."

"But how could you? What is it?" Peter asked grimly.

"It's a diminutive of Importuna."

"Diminutive. You mean like Import? Look,

Virgin, you're trying to sidetrack me —"

"Shorter than that." Something kept egging me on. A demon, what else? No other explanation is sane.

"Shorter than Import? . . . Imp? That's about as appropriate for him as Cuddles would be."

"In between," I said. You know. Sprightly. A little boy-girl game. How stupid can you get?

"In between Import and Imp." Peter's blond-silk brows made like a frown. "You're putting me on. There's nothing between Import and Imp."

"Oh, no?" Big Mouth babbles. "How about Impo?"

The moment I said it I'd have bitten my tongue off at the roots if my teeth could have reached that far. Because what it gave Peter was newborn hope. I saw the infant burst into life in his eyes, ready to yell.

"Impo!" he said. "You can't mean Nino — the great Nino — is incapable of . . . ?"

"It's not worth discussing," I said, fast. "I don't know why I brought it up. Don't you think we'd better order?"

"Not worth *discussing?*"

"Peter, keep your voice down. *Please.*"

"My God, baby, don't you know what this means? If your marriage has never been consummated, it's not a real marriage. That's grounds for an annulment!"

In his exuberance Peter didn't think to pursue the subject of exactly what my marital life did consist of. Which was just as well. I don't want to think of what might have happened. It turned out badly enough as it is.

So I went through the whole dreary recitation of no-noes. How it didn't matter what I could or couldn't do to have the marriage dissolved, legally, religiously, or any other way if such existed — how because of daddy Nino had me by the short hairs, now more than ever, because the Gay Controller had *not* learned his lesson in 1962, the lesson I've already paid for with almost five years of my life. Although he hasn't dipped into the till again and played more hanky-pank with the books — Nino's made sure of that — he hasn't stopped plunging on speculative stocks in the market or betting on long shots at the track, either. He keeps losing and going into debt to the loan sharks and Nino, kind, generous Nino, keeps bailing him out . . . his *suocero,* his father-in-law, his beloved's papa. Never failing to give me an accounting to the penny, so that I'll know the rising score of my obligation to him, and what he's still holding over dad's and my head: that's fitting for a prison uniform.

"How can I let that happen, Peter? He is my father, the only one I'll ever have. In his own cockeyed way he loves me. Anyway, we couldn't build a life on a foundation like that. I know I couldn't, and I don't believe you could, either."

"I'm not so sure about that," Peter said crassly. "What's the matter with that crazy old man of yours? Why the hell doesn't he start seeing a psychiatrist? Doesn't he realize he's ruining your life?"

"He's a compulsive gambler, Peter."

"And womanizer — let's not forget *that*. Virgin, your father is a compulsive everything." Peter's been calling me Virgin in private for some time now, how aptly he hasn't known. It makes me writhe. "You say he loves you. It's a hell of a love that makes a father sell his only daughter to a — a eunuch just to save his own miserable hide!"

"Daddy's weak, Peter, and self-indulgent, and all the rest of it, but he really doesn't think marrying me off to one of the world's richest men is such a horrible fate. Of course, he doesn't know about Nino's . . . condition." The waiter was hanging about, and I said haughtily, "I'm hungry," which I was not. "Are you trying to starve me?"

We ordered something, I think mine was a veal cutlet that had been breaded in library paste — their marvelous chef must have been off today — and Peter kept asking me district attorney-type questions about the agreement I had been forced to sign before the wedding. I suppose he was desperate, poor darling, because we'd been over *that* Berlin wall a dozen times previously without finding a loophole or the sorriest chink. I had to point out to him again that for the five-year term of the agreement I have absolutely no financial claim on Nino or his estate, and if I left his bed (!) and board before the expiration date it would not only strand me without a Hungarian pengö but he could — and positively would — sic the gendarmes on daddy and have him packed off to jail on the old embezzlement charge.

"Is his money so important to you?" How Peter's lip curled.

"I hate it. *And* him! For Pete's sake, Peter, you can't really think it's the money. I *told* you. I'd gladly accept any kind of decent life, no matter how much of a struggle it would be, if not for —"

"Right back to dear old dad again," Peter said, grinding his teeth. "Oh, damn him! When's the due date?"

"Of what, Peter?"

"The agreement. When the five years are up. That's one of Nino's private papers he's never let me in on."

"What's today? December 9. Well, it expires 9 months from today, on Nino's 68th birthday, which is also our fifth anniversary. September 9 next year."

"Nine months," Peter said in a very peculiar way.

I hadn't realized till Peter repeated it, and it struck me funny, so I laughed. Peter did not, and at the expression on his face I didn't feel like laughing anymore. "What's the matter now, Peter? What is it?"

He said, "Nothing."

The way he said it . . .

I know it was definitely not nothing. It was *something*. Something terrible. I mean what was going through that blond, frustrated, furious head. I didn't even want to think about what it might be. I wanted to wipe it out of *my* head just as fast as I possibly could. I told myself my Peter couldn't be thinking unthinkable thoughts like that. Even in fury. Or fantasy. Or anything.

But I knew he could. And was.

Does one ever really dig another human being? Not excluding the man one loves? And I mean dig? In every sense?

At that moment I didn't know Mr. P. Ennis, 30, Harvard '59, confidential secretary to Nino Importuna, Julio Importunato, and Marco Importunato, in charge of the three brothers' personal affairs . . . I didn't know him from any stranger brushed against in the street.

It frightened me.

It still does.

And that wasn't all that made today so bitchy. As I was staring across the table at Peter, biting on my napkin, I saw over his shoulder — just walking into the restaurant — my father. At the moment I spotted him I noticed a flashy chick near him, but whether she was with him or coming in alone I never did find out. The big thing that concerned me was that he mustn't see me with Peter. Because not even daddy knows about Peter and me. He'd never consciously betray me to Nino, but he does take a few drinks too many sometimes, and Nino is a breathing radar — he plucks information out of empty air. I simply couldn't risk it.

I said under my breath to Peter, "Peter, there's my father — no, don't look — he mustn't see us together . . . !"

Bless Peter. He casually dropped a $20 bill on the table and strolled me toward the rear, so that our backs were to daddy all the way. We pretended to go to the rest rooms but instead we escaped through an utterly blasé kitchen staff. There's not much you can do to make New York service people look up from their appointed chores short of planting a bomb under them.

It was a close call, too close, and I told Peter outside that we didn't dare rendezvous in public again. He took one look at my stricken face, kissed me, and put me into a cab.

But my love wasn't through with me. Oh, no! just before he slammed the cab door Peter said in a low, throbby sort of voice, "There's only one thing for me to do and, by God, when the time is ripe I'm going to do it."

That was the last I've seen of him today.

But that remark of Peter's has been haunting me. That, and the look on his face a few moments before daddy walked into the restaurant.

9 months . . .

It's as if something was conceived today in the womb of time. I hope and pray I'm wrong, because if I glimpsed in Peter's eyes what I think I glimpsed, and if his parting shot to me meant what I think it meant, the embryo's going to turn out to be a thalidomide baby, or worse.

It's a very morbid thought, and I'm becoming incoherent besides. I see I've finished over half the fifth of zatsomac, and I'm good and smashed, which I almost never allow myself to get because I might grow to like it too much, and to hell with you and you and you too Mrs. Calabash. I'd better totter off and tuck my lil ole self into beddy-snooky-bye.

FIRST
MONTH

January, 1967

Gestation, the carrying or bearing, has begun.

The zygote has become a multicelled embryo. It has grown to the size of a pea and its core to the size of a pinhead.

The cells in this core now form a ridge, at one end of which an infinitesimal knob takes shape. It is the beginning of the head.

SECOND
MONTH

February, 1967

Before the latter part of the second month it is not possible, from ordinary observation, to determine whether the embryo is of a human being or a dog.

But after the first eight weeks, it takes on the unmistakable semblance of humanity.

By now it is no longer an embryo.

It is a fetus.

THIRD
MONTH

March, 1967

The eyes are no longer on the sides of the head but have approached each other. Tiny slits mark the ears and nostrils, a larger slit marks the mouth. The forehead has grown massive. The upper limbs show fingers, wrists, forearms. The internal reproductive organs can now be distinguished as to sex.

FOURTH MONTH

April, 1967

During this period the abdomen develops with notable rapidity, reducing the disproportion between the head and the rest of the fetus.

Hair emerges on the head.

The mother begins to feel the stir of her little parasite.

FIFTH
MONTH

May, 1967

The halfway stage of the pregnancy finds the lower portion of the fetus's abdomen enlarging proportionately, and the legs beginning to catch up.

The mother is now very much aware of what she is bearing. Its arms and legs are in frequent vigorous motion in her body.

Ellery had had his study done over in driftwood paneling, a choice that had seemed inspired at the time. The pitted and irregularly furrowed surface looked as if it had been clawed by the tides of years, and it was artistically stained a salty sea-foam gray. Contemplating it, he could feel the rise and fall of his floor and little imaginary stings on his cheeks. With the air conditioner set to maximum, it was very hard to keep reminding himself that he was not on the deck of a pleasure craft plowing up the Sound.

This proved a serious deterrent to the requirements of reality. The conversion of his workaday walls had altered his environment to the critical point, turning a functional study in an ordinary Manhattan apartment into a playful distraction. Ellery had always held that, for the most efficient use of time and the maintenance of a schedule, a writer required above all things a working atmosphere of familiar discomfort. One should never change so much as the Model T pencil sharpener on the windowsill. The very grime around the ratholes was an encouragement to labor. In the ancient metaphor, the creative flame burned brightest in dark and dusty garrets; and so forth.

Why had he excommunicated the dear old

dirty wallpaper that had seen him devotedly through so many completed manuscripts?

He was glaring at the four and a half sentences in his typewriter and making beseeching motions with his hands when his father looked in, said, "Still working?" in a tired voice, and retreated from the sight of that anguished tableau.

Five minutes later, somewhat refreshed and bearing a frosty, green-tinged cocktail, the old man reappeared. Ellery was now smiting himself softly on the temple.

Inspector Queen sank onto Ellery's sofa, taking a thirsty swallow on the way down. "Why keep beating your brains in?" he demanded. "Knock it off, son. You've got less on that page than when I left for downtown this morning."

"What?" Ellery said, not looking up.

"Call it a day."

Ellery looked up. "Never. Can't. Way behind."

"You'll make it up."

He burped a hollow laugh. "Dad, I'm trying to work. Mind?"

The Inspector settled himself and held up his cocktail. "How about I make you one of these?"

"What?"

"I said," the Inspector said patiently, "would you like a Tipperary? It's a Doc Prouty special."

"What's in it?" Ellery asked, making a micrometric adjustment of the sheet in his machine, which was already adjusted to a hun-

51

dredth of an inch. "I've sampled Doc Prouty specials before, and they all taste the way his lab smells. What's the green stuff?"

"Chartreuse. Mixed with Irish whiskey and sweet vermouth."

"No crème de menthe? God keep us all from professional Irishmen! If you're bent on bar-keeping, dad, make mine a Johnnie on the rocks."

His father fetched the Scotch. Ellery surrounded half of it with sedate gratitude, set the glass daintily down beside his typewriter, and flexed his fingers. The old man sat back on the sofa, knees touching like a vicar's on duty call, sipping his Tipperary and watching. Just as the poised filial fingers were about to descend on the keys, the paterfamilias said, "Yes, sir. Hell of a day."

The son slowly lowered his hands. He sat back. He reached for his glass. "All right," he said. "I'm listening."

"No, no, I just happened to think out loud, son. It's not important. I mean, sorry I interrupted."

"So am I, but the fact, as de Gaulle would say in translation, is accomplished. I couldn't compose a printable line now if I were on my deathbed."

"I said I was sorry," the Inspector said in a huff. "I see I'd better get out of here."

"Oh, sit down. You obviously invaded my domain with malice aforeceps, as a show biz lady of my acquaintance liked to say, in contravention of my rights under the Fourth Amendment." The old man sat back, rather bewilderedly mollified. "By the way, how about not talking on an empty stomach? Dinner simmers on the hod. Mrs. Fabrikant left us one of her famous, or to put it more accurately, notorious Irish stews. Fabby had to leave early today —"

"I'm in no hurry to eat," the Inspector said hurriedly.

"Done! I'll run down to Sammy's later for some hot kosher pastrami and Jewish rye and lots of half-sour pickles and stuff, and we can feed Fabby's stew to the Delehantys' setter, he's Irish —"

"Fine, fine."

"Therefore how about another round?" Ellery struggled to the vertical, revived a few moribund muscles and tendons, shook himself, and then came round the desk with his glass. He took his father's empty from the slack fingers. "You still traveling that long way?"

"Long way?"

"To Tipperary. Proportions?"

"Three-quarters of an ounce each of Irish, sweet vermouth, and —"

"I know, green chartreuse." He shuddered (the Inspector snapped, "Very funny!") and dodged into the living room. When he returned, instead of reoccupying his desk chair Ellery dropped into the overstuffed chair facing the sofa.

"If it's ambulatory help you need, dad, I can't lift my duff. That damn deadline's so close the back of my neck is recommending Listerine. But if you can use an armchair opinion . . . What's this one about?"

"About a third of a half billion dollars," Inspector Queen grunted. "And you don't have to be so darn merry about it."

"It's frustrated-writer's hysteria, dad. Did I hear you correctly? *Bill*ion?"

"Right. With a buh."

"For pity land's sake. Who's involved?"

"Importuna Industries. Know anything about the outfit?"

"Only that it's a conglomerate of a whole slew of industries and companies, great and small, foreign and domestic, the entire *shtik* owned by three brothers named Importuna."

"Wrong."

"Wrong?"

"Owned by *one* brother named Importuna. The other two carry the handle Importunato."

"Full brothers? Or half, or step?"

"Full, far as I know."

"How come the difference in surnames?"

"Nino, the oldest, is superstitious, has a thing about lucky numbers or something — I had more important things to break my head about. Anyway, he shortened the family name. His brothers didn't."

"Noted. Well?"

"Oh, hell," his father said, and swigged like a

desperate man. "Ellery, I warn you . . . this is wild. I don't want to be responsible for dragging you into a complicated mess when you've your own work to do. . . ."

"You're absolved, dad, shriven. But put it in writing if you like. Satisfied? Go on!"

"Well, all right," the Inspector said, with an on-your-head-be-it sigh. "The three brothers live in an apartment house they own on the upper East Side, overlooking the river. It's an old-timer, 9 stories and penthouse, designed by somebody important in the late '90s, and when Nino Importuna bought it, he had it restored to its original condition, modernized the plumbing and heating, installed the latest in air conditioning, and so on — turned it into one of the snootiest buildings in the neighborhood. I understand that prospective tenants have to go through a tougher check than the security men assigned to the President."

"I gather not quite," Ellery suggested.

"I'm coming to that. The place is one of I don't know how many homes the brothers maintain around the world — especially Nino — but 99 East, as Importuna calls it, seems to be the one they run the conglomerate from, at least the American components."

"Don't they have offices?"

"Offices? Whole chains of office buildings! But the real dirty work, the high command decisions, that all originates at 99 East. — Okay, Ellery! But before I can get to the murder —"

At the lethal word Ellery's nose twitched like a Saint Bernard's. "Can't you at least tell me who was schlogged? How? Where?"

"If you'll wait just a minute, Son! The setup's as follows: Nino occupies the penthouse. His brothers Marco and Julio live in the apartments that make up the top floor of the building, the floor directly underneath the penthouse — there are two apartments to a floor except on the roof, and they're enormous, I don't know how many rooms to an apartment. You know those swanky old buildings.

"Now the brothers share the services of a confidential secretary, a fellow named Ennis, Peter Ennis, good-looking guy who's got to be mighty sharp or he wouldn't be holding down a job like that —"

"Confidential secretary could cover a lot of territory. Just what does Ennis handle for the brothers?"

"Their personal affairs mostly, he says, although of course, with the brothers operating so much from their homes I don't see how Ennis could fail to get in on some of the business shenanigans, too. Anyway, this morning, early —"

"Are all the brothers married?"

"Nino. The other two are single. Do you want me to get to the murder or don't you?"

"I'm nothing but ears."

"When Ennis showed up for work this morning, he made his rounds of the three apartments, he says, the way he always does, to get squared away for the day. He found Julio, who's the youngest brother, dead. Bloody dead — a real mess."

"*Where* did he find him?"

"In Julio's apartment, the library there. Importunato had his head beaten in. I mean he was zonked. Just one sock, but it was a beaut — clobbered his brains into mush. On that side, anyway. It's a nasty homicide, Ellery, and considering the murderee is one of the ruling dynasty of the Importuna empire, it's a sizzler. The shock waves . . ." Inspector Queen gulped generously.

"What shock waves?"

"Didn't you listen to the six o'clock news?"

"I haven't turned the radio on all week. What happened?"

"Julio Importunato's murder rocked the stock market. Not only Wall Street — the money markets of Europe, too. That was the first aftereffect. The second came down from the commissioner. He's putting the squeeze on, son — so is the mayor — and I'm one of those caught between the nut-crackers."

"Damn." Ellery shafted a malevolent glance at his stubborn typewriter. "And? Well?"

"On second thought, what's the point? It's no use, Ellery. You go on back to your work." The Inspector made a rather theatrical move to rise. "I'll manage. Somehow."

"You know, you can be an exasperating old man!" Ellery exclaimed. "What do you mean, it's no use? There's always a 'use'! But I can't be of use if you keep me in ignorance. What are the facts? Are there any clues?"

"Oh. Well, yes. At least two." He stopped.

"And?" Ellery snapped after a while. "Specify!"

"In fact," the Inspector replied joylessly, "they both point straight at the killer."

"They do? At whom?"

"Marco."

"His *brother?*"

"Right."

"Then what's the problem? I don't understand, dad. You're acting as if you're stumped, and in the same breath you say you have a couple of clues that link the victim's brother directly to the crime!"

"That's correct."

"But . . . For heaven's sake, what kind of clues are they?"

"The open-and-shut kind. The real old-fashioned variety, you'd have to call 'em. The kind," Inspector Queen said, shaking his mustache, "you mystery writers wouldn't be caught dead putting in one of your stories in this day and age."

"All right, you've whipped my interest to a bloody froth," Ellery said in a grim voice. "Now let's get down to cases. What — precisely — are these open-and-shut, old-fashioned, downright corny clues?"

"From the condition in which we found Julio's

library, there'd been a fight, a violent struggle. Real donnybrook. Well, we found on the scene a button —"

"What kind of button?"

"Solid gold. Monogram *MI* on it."

"Identified as Marco Importunato's?"

"Identified as Marco Importunato's. Threads still hanging from it. That's clue the first."

"Button," Ellery repeated. "Buttons-found-on-scene-of-crime went out with spats and Hoover collars. And the other clue?"

"Went out with zoot suits."

"But what is it?"

Inspector Queen said, "A footprint."

"Footprint! You mean of a naked foot?"

"Of a shoe. A man's shoe."

"Where was it found?"

"Dead man's library. Scene of the homicide."

"But . . . And you tied the print into Marco?"

"We sure did."

"A button and a footprint," Ellery said, marveling. "In the year 1967! Well, I suppose anything's possible. A time warp, or something. But if it's that pat, dad, what's bothering you?"

"It isn't that pat."

"But I thought you said —"

"I told you. It's very complicated."

"Complicated how? By what?"

The old man set his empty glass on the floor, where presumably it could be more conveniently kicked. Ellery watched him with sharpening suspicion.

"I'm sincerely sorry I told you anything about it," his father said sincerely, and rose. "Let's forget it, son. I mean, you forget it."

"Thanks a heap! How do I do that? It's apparently one of those lovely deceptive ones that only appears to be a simple case. Therefore . . ."

The "Yes?" came out of the Inspector's birdy face like an impatient twitter.

"I've suddenly come down with a recurrence of my old enteric fever. You know, dad, the aftermath of the jezail bullet that grazed my subclavian artery and shattered my shoulder at the battle of Maiwand?"

"Shattered your shoulder?" his father cried. "What bullet grazed your artery? At which battle?"

"I'll consequently have to notify my publisher that there will be a slight delay in the delivery of my next book. After all, what difference can it make to anyone there? It's probably wandering around somewhere on their schedule, hopelessly lost. Nobody in the publishing profession pays any attention whatever to a mystery writer except when banking the profits from his mean endeavors. We're the ditchdiggers of literature."

"Ellery, I don't want to be the cause of —"

"You've already said that. Of course you do, or you'd have swallowed a few mouthfuls of Fabby's well-meant swill and crept into bed without my being aware you'd even come home. And why not? There are heavyweight VIPs involved, the crunch is on downtown, you're not getting any younger, and did I ever leave you in the lurch? Now let's get to it."

"You really want to, son?"

"I thought I'd just said so."

A beautiful change came over Inspector Queen. The relief map of his face turned into a map of relief.

"In that case," he cried, "you get your jacket!"

Ellery rose to oblige. "Where to?"

"Lab."

A sergeant, Joe Voytershack, one of the Technical Services Bureau's most reliable men, was on overtime duty tonight, by which Ellery gauged the importance of the case in the eyes of the budget-conscious brass. Sergeant Voytershack was studying a button under his loupe. The button was of gold, and a clump of navy blue threads protruded from it.

"What's the problem, Joe?" Inspector Queen asked. "I thought you'd finished with the button."

"I had."

"Then why are you examining it again?"

"Because," Sergeant Voytershack said sourly, "I'm goddam unhappy about it. Because I don't like this button. Because I don't like it from *bupkes*. And I don't see *you* leaping for joy, either, Inspector."

"Ellery wants a look."

"Hello, Joe," Ellery said.

"Be my guest." The sergeant handed him the

loupe and the button.

Ellery peered.

"I thought, dad, you said this button was torn off during a struggle."

"Did I say that?"

"Not exactly. But I naturally assumed —"

"I think you're going to find out, my son," Inspector Queen said, "that in this case assumptions are kind of risky. What I said was that there were indications of a violent struggle, which there are, and that we found a gold button on the scene, which we did. I didn't say one necessarily had to do with the other. Just for ducks, Ellery: What do you see?"

"I see a clump of threads of identical length, with very sharp, clean ends. If the button had been yanked off during a struggle — that is, by hand — the lengths of the threads would vary and the ends, instead of being sharp and clean, would be ragged. This button was snipped off whatever it was attached to by a sharp-edged instrument, a scissors or knife, more likely a scissors."

"Right," said Sergeant Voytershack.

"Right," said Inspector Queen.

"Was it found in the dead man's hands?"

"It was found on the dead man's floor."

Ellery shrugged. "Not that it would change the picture if you'd found it in his hand. The fact is, someone cut this button off something belonging to Marco Importunato. Since it was found on the scene of the murder, the indicated conclusion is that it was planted there for the benefit of you gents of the fuzz. Somebody doesn't care for Brother Marco, either."

"Yes, sir, you just hit a couple of nails," his father said. "Turning what looked at first like a nice clean clue against Marco into a dirty frame-up of Marco. See? Simple into not so simple."

Ellery scowled. He picked the button up by its rim and turned it over. The relief design on its face formed a conventional frame of crossed anchors and hawsers, with the initials *MI* in an elaborate intertwine engraved within the frame.

He set the button down and turned to the technical man. "Was a cast made from the shoeprint, sergeant? I'd like to see it."

Voytershack shook his grizzled head. "Didn't the Inspector describe it to you?"

"Didn't tell him a bloody thing about it," the old man said. "I don't want to influence his impressions."

The sergeant handed Ellery a number of photographs. They were largely close-ups, from various angles, of the same object, which was lying on what appeared to be a short-piled rug.

"What is that material the shoeprint shows up on?" Ellery asked. "Looks like ashes."

"It is ashes," Voytershack said.

"What kind?"

"Cigar."

There was a great deal of it. In one picture, taken at slightly longer range, a large glass ashtray in what seemed to be an ebony holder was visible on the rug a foot or so from the ash deposit. The ashtray lay face down.

"Whose cigars?" Ellery asked. "Do you have a make on that?"

"They're from the same cigars the boys found in a humidor on the murdered guy's desk," the sergeant said. "Prime Cuban. The finest."

"The tray must have been piled pretty high to have dumped this much ash when it over-turned."

"They all claim Julio was a cigar chain-smoker," Inspector Queen said. "And the maid hadn't yet cleaned up his library this morning from yesterday."

"So presumably the tray was knocked off the desk in the struggle?"

"That's the way it figures. Joe'll show you the series of photos of the room. Chairs and lamps knocked over, a 200-year old Chinese vase smashed to bits, a rack of fire tools upset — one of them, a hefty three-foot trident-type poker, was the murder weapon — an antique taboret squashed to kindling wood where somebody must have fallen on it — as I told you back home, a donnybrook. What do you make of the shoe-print, Ellery?"

"Man's right shoe, smallish size — I'd esti-mate no more than an eight, could even be a seven. The sole is rippled. Might be of crepe. Certainly a sports shoe of some type. Also, diagonally down the length of the sole there's something that looks like a deep cut in the crepe.

It's definitely not part of the design of the sole. The cut crosses four consecutive ripples of the crepe at an acute angle. Dad, this should have made identification a kindergarten exercise. That is, if you found the shoe."

"Oh, it was, and we did," the Inspector said. "The shoe — a yachting slice, by the way, and crepe-soled, as you say — was found on the 9th floor of 99 East, in a shoe rack of the east apartment's dressing room adjoining the master bedroom. Size about 7½C. Fits the imprint in the ashes like a glove. And with a cut in the sole positioned exactly as in the ashes, crossing the same four ripples at the same angle."

"Marco Importunato's apartment. His shoe."

"Marco's apartment, his shoe. Right."

"Joe, do you have the shoe here?"

Sergeant Voytershack produced it. It was a common navy blue sports oxford with the characteristic thick crepe sole. Ellery studied the crosscut.

"May I have a caliper or a tongs, Joe — something to pry the edges of the cut apart?"

Voytershack handed him a tool and a magnifying glass. The two officers watched without expression. Ellery separated the lips of the cut and peered into its vitals through the glass.

He looked up with a nod. "Can't be much doubt. The cut down the sole looks fresh — definitely not an old cut; in fact, it was made very recently. And I don't see how a slash of this length and uniform depth could have been the result of stepping on something, unless the wearer of the shoe was doing a balancing act on an ax blade. So the cut across these ripples in the crepe was made deliberately. And since this is a mass-produced sports shoe obtainable almost anywhere, making it hard to trace, the purpose of the cut can only have been for identification — to connect the distinctive print the shoe left in the cigar ashes with the specific shoe belonging to Marco Importunato. In other words — again — to frame Marco for his brother Julio's murder. Has Marco been questioned yet?"

"Very delicately," Inspector Queen said. "Sort of in passing. In this case, we decided, haste makes headaches. We're sort of feeling our way around."

Ellery set Marco Importunato's shoe down. Sergeant Voytershack carefully stowed it away.

"And that's the extent of the case against Marco?" Ellery asked. "The gold button? The shoeprint?"

His father said, "He's also left-handed."

"Left-handed? Impossible. Nobody stoops to using left-handed murderers anymore."

"In mystery stories."

"There's a clue to left-handedness?"

"Not exactly."

"What's that supposed to mean?"

"The crime could have been committed by a left-handed man."

"And I suppose all the other suspects are right-handed?"

"I don't know about all the suspects — 'all' covers a lot of ground, and we haven't even scratched the surface of the potentials. For what it's worth, Marco's brothers, Julio who was the victim and Nino who heads the whole shebang, were . . . are . . . whatever the devil it is! — both right-handed."

"Why do you say the crime could have been committed by a southpaw? Where's the clue to that?"

Inspector Queen's chin jerked at the sergeant. In silence Voytershack handed Ellery a portfolio of photographs.

The Inspector tapped the uppermost photo. "You tell me."

It showed a corner of a room.

The picture was not a sample of the lensman's art by any criterion of esthetics. There was a long desk, heavy-looking, with an oak grain in a feudal finish, extensively carved. A man, or what had been a man, was seated in what appeared to be a swivel chair, midway behind the desk. The view was from across the desk, facing the dead man. The upper torso and head lay fallen forward on the desk top, and one side of the head was caved in.

The large desk blotter and some papers scattered on the desk — fortuitously, one of them on the squashed side was a newspaper — had sopped up most of the blood and brain matter. That entire side — of the head, the shoulder, the desk — was a continuous ruin.

"From the wound," Ellery said, making a face, "a single blow, a crusher; had to have been full arm. A home run in any park." He snapped a fingertip at the color print. "Question: If there was a battle royal between Julio and his killer of sufficient violence to shatter vases and break furniture, how come Julio was found seated more or less peaceably behind the desk?"

"We have to figure he lost the fight," the Inspector said with a shrug. "Killer then forced him to sit down behind the desk, or conned him into it, on what excuse or threat or sweet talk is anybody's guess. Maybe to talk over their differences, whatever they were . . . I mean why they fought in the first place. However the killer managed it, it led to his crowning Julio with the poker. It's the only theory that makes sense to us. If any of this makes sense."

"Any fix on the time of the murder? Did Prouty's man say?"

"Prouty's man? Are you kidding? This one was important enough to bring the eminent Dr. Prouty trotting out in the flesh. Last night around 10 P.M. is Doc's preliminary estimate."

"Didn't anyone hear the fight?"

"The servants' quarters are way to hell and gone at the other end of Julio's apartment, which goes on forever. And as far as overhearing is concerned, you could stage a kid gang rumble in one of those rooms and nobody'd know it. They built walls that were walls in the days when 99 East was put up, not the cardboard partitions they use today. No, nobody heard the fight."

Ellery set the photograph down. Sergeant Voytershack reached for it. But Ellery had already picked it up again. "And Prouty couldn't be more exact about the time?"

"Restless, my son?" his father asked. "Doesn't this case come up to your usual standard? No, Doc couldn't — not today, anyway. He says he'll give us, quote, 'a more accurate stab in the dark,' unquote, as soon as he can. If he can."

"You don't seem to have much confidence in anything about the case."

"And you," Inspector Queen retorted, "don't seem in much of a hurry to hold forth on the left-handedness business."

Ellery scowled and squinted at the photograph. One of the short ends of the desk met the side wall. The desk's long dimension was therefore parallel with the rear wall, the one behind the dead man's chair.

"No mystery about it," Ellery said. "Certainly not from this photo. From the position and angle of the line of impact made on this side of the skull by the weapon, assuming that when Julio was struck he was sitting up normally in the chair, the blow could certainly have been delivered by a left-handed man."

The Inspector and Sergeant Voytershack nodded without enthusiasm.

"That's it?" Inspector Queen asked.

"Not to me it isn't," Ellery said. "Not yet. It's consistent with Marco's left-handedness, all right, but that may be the trouble. If Marco's being framed, if the button and shoe-print were plants, this left-handedness possibility may be a plant, too. I'd like to see Julio's library close up, dad. And can you arrange to have the confidential secretary — what's his name? Peter Ennis? — join us there?"

It was 9:35 P.M. when the Queens rode the small private elevator to the top floor of 99 East and stepped out into the modest vestibule that served both the east and west 9th-floor apartments. They had had to struggle through the wasps' nest of reporters and photographers downstairs, and both men were ruffled.

"Open up," Inspector Queen snapped to the officer on guard at the east door. The man rapped three times, and the door was unlocked from inside by another officer.

"Bad down there, Inspector?" he asked.

"It's as much as your life is worth. It's all right, Mulvey, we'll find it. I have hound-dog blood in me."

Ellery followed his father, taking in the high ceilings and rococo ornamentation of the apartment. The furniture was ponderous and for the most part Italian, but the décor was haphazardly bright, expressing no particular scheme or period but rather the whims of the decorator, undoubtedly Julio Importunato himself. The murdered man, Ellery reflected, must have been a lighthearted, chromatic *amante* of life. The life-sized oil portrait in the living room through which they passed confirmed his guess. It was of a large, doughy man with a lusty mustache and eyes that reminded him of a Hals he had seen in the Louvre. *The Gypsy*, brimming over with amiable mischief. The portraitist's symbolism was as hearty as the subject himself. On the table at which the artist had painted the youngest brother lay an overturned leather dicebox with the dice spilled out beside an empty bottle of *vino;* a slopping wineglass was clutched in the fist resting on the table. And, reflected in a background mirror (the curlicued frame was festooned with gold cupids) on an opulent bed, lay a smiling woman of noble dimensions with one rosy leg drawn up and no clothes on.

"Pity," Ellery said.

"What?"

"I was having a platitudinous thought about death. An epitaph for Julio. How many rooms are there in this labyrinth, anyway?"

They finally penetrated to the scene of the murder. The library, Inspector Queen said, was in the same condition as when Peter Ennis had found the dead man, except for what had necessarily been disturbed in the police workover. Chairs were overturned, lamps lay broken on the floor, the rack of fire tools at the fireplace sprawled on the hearthstone; even the débris of the antique taboret lay where it had collapsed. And while Julio Importunato's body was no longer there, its surrogate remained — the ghostly outline of his torso and head chalked on the bloodied desk.

"That's where the shoeprint was?" Ellery pointed with his toe to an erratic hole some two feet in diameter in the cobalt blue Indian rug. The piece had been cut out of the rug near one of the front corners of the desk.

Inspector Queen nodded. "For the D.A.'s office." He added, "Hopefully."

"That's the name of this game. Is Ennis here?"

The Inspector nodded to the patrolman on duty and the patrolman opened a door at the far end of the library. Two men came in. The man who appeared first could not have been Ennis in any event; he strolled, in no hurry, the captain of a ship, unquestioned master of his decks. Peter Ennis followed with quick small steps, in a sort of choreography, the very model of the subordinate; the small steps shrank his natural advantage of height over his employer to their real proportions.

"This is Mr. Importuna," the younger man announced. "Mr. Nino Importuna." He possessed a surprising high tenor voice, incongruous in a man of his size and virile blond appearance.

No one acknowledged the fanfare; Ennis took one step back, flushing.

Importuna stopped before his murdered brother's desk, surveying the dried blood, the bits of tissue, the chalked outline. Whatever he felt, he did not allow it to show.

"This is the first time I've seen" — his right hand with its four fingers described a vague oval — "this. They wouldn't let me in before."

"You shouldn't be here now, Mr. Importuna," Inspector Queen said. "I'd rather have spared you this."

"Kind but not necessary," the multimillionaire said. His voice sounded deep and dry, with a faint echo of remorse, like an abandoned well. "Italian *contadini* are used to the sight of blood. . . . So this is how the murder of a brother looks. *Omicidio a sangue freddo.*"

"Why do you say 'in cold blood,' Mr. Importuna?" Ellery asked.

The adversary eyes turned Ellery's way. They took his measure. "Who are you? You're not a policeman."

"My son Ellery," the Inspector said, quickly. "He has a professional interest in homicide, Mr. Importuna, though his profession isn't police work. He writes about it."

"Oh? My brother Julio becomes your raw material, Mr. Queen?"

"Not for profit," Ellery said. "We have the feeling this is a difficult case, Mr. Importuna. I'm helping out. But you haven't answered my question."

"You understand Italian?"

"A very little. Why in cold blood?"

"One stroke of the weapon, I understand. Directed with great force and precision. That is not the work of anger or blind hatred. If my

73

brother had been attacked in passion, there would have been not one blow but many."

"You should be a detective, Mr. Importuna," Ellery said. "You've just made a most important observation."

Nino Importuna shrugged. "By the way, gentlemen, I apologize for the failure of my wife to make an appearance. Mrs. Importuna was very fond of Julio. His murder has so affected her I've had to forbid her to set foot in his apartment."

"We'll have to talk to her, of course," Inspector Queen said. "But there's no hurry, Mr. Importuna. At your wife's convenience."

"Thank you. I understand you want to question my secretary again? Mr. Ennis here?"

"My son wants to."

"Peter, tell Mr. Queen whatever he wants to know."

The heavyset man retreated to the nearest wall. There was a chair nearby, but he leaned against the wall. His womanish mouth was compressed. He kept his eyes on Ennis.

"I suppose," Peter Ennis said to Ellery, "you want me to repeat my story — I mean how I came to find —"

"No," Ellery said.

"No?"

"No, I'd like you to tell me what your impressions were, Mr. Ennis, when you got over the first shock of finding Mr. Importunato murdered."

"I'm afraid," the blond secretary stammered,

"I'm afraid I don't exactly understand what you . . ."

Ellery smiled at him. "I don't blame you for being confused. I'm not quite sure myself what I'm groping for. Let's try this: Was there anything about the room at that time that struck you, well, as different from usual? I understand you're familiar with all three apartments. Sometimes on entering familiar surroundings we get an uneasy feeling, a sense of disturbance, because something is out of place, or missing, or even added."

"Of course, the overturned things, this broken stuff —"

"Aside from those, Mr. Ennis."

"Well . . ."

"One moment."

To Inspector Queen's eye Ellery was at the old point, like the bird dog he often resembled. He was almost quivering, he stood so still. He was concentrating his attention on something in the rug, about halfway between the end of the desk jutting into the room and the rear wall.

Suddenly he ran over to it, dropped to one knee, and studied it at close range. Then he scuttled over to a point well behind the desk, near the base of the rear wall, and intently examined something there. Whereupon he sprang to his feet, ran around to the front of the desk, got down on all fours, and peered underneath at a point about one-third the desk's length from the side wall.

This time when he rose he beckoned the patrolman.

"Would you help me, please?"

He directed the officer to lift the desk at its front corner, the corner nearest the side wall. "Just an inch or so. A little higher. That's it. Hold it a moment." He peered closely at the rug directly below the corner leg. "Fine. Now over here."

He had the patrolman repeat the procedure at each of the other corners of the desk. His examination at the rear corner beside the side wall took a little longer.

Finally he nodded to the patrolman and rose.

"Well?" There was no expectation of surprise in the Inspector's voice.

Ellery glanced over at Ennis and Importuna. His father replied with the slightest nod. Ellery promptly returned to his original point of survey. "If you'll examine the rug here," he said, "you'll see a circular depression in it, of the same diameter as the end of one of these desk legs, but on a spot where no desk leg stands. On the other hand, if you raise the nearest corner of the desk and examine the rug where a leg *is* standing, you find a curious thing: the depression there is not nearly as deep as the one where no leg stands.

"Over here" — and Ellery proceeded to his second point of examination, behind the desk and almost at the base of the rear wall — "exactly the same phenomenon; a very deep depression where no desk leg now stands but where obviously one did stand for a long time. And where a corresponding leg actually does stand, there's a much shallower depression.

"Go around to the front of the desk, a short way from the side wall, and partway under the desk you'll see another deep depression, whereas the rug under the nearest leg to it shows the shallower depression, too.

"And if you examine the rug under the rear leg nearest the side wall, you discover the most interesting phenomenon of all: not a shallow depression, as where the other three legs now stand, but one even deeper than the other deep impressions! As if, in fact, that leg had been used as a pivot.

"The only possible conclusion," Ellery said, "is that the desk was moved — shifted from where it usually stood to where it stands now. And, judging from the shallowness of the depressions under the legs in their present position, it was shifted very recently."

"So?" the Inspector said in the same unmoved way.

"So let's use the deep depressions as guides — Officer, would you mind grabbing hold of the end of the desk here? — and, pivoting the desk on that rear leg at the side wall, let's set it down exactly on the deep depressions — no, a bit more, Officer; that's it — and we've got the desk back to where it customarily stands . . . catercornered, as you see, with the swivel chair virtually boxed in in what's now a triangular space behind the desk. Leaving hardly enough room at either end for anyone to get behind it. In fact, it must have been a tight squeeze for Mr. Importunato, with his bulk, when he wanted to sit down there. Isn't that so, Mr. Ennis?"

Peter Ennis's embarrassment was embarrassing. "I really don't know what to say, Mr. Queen. Of course this is the way the desk's always stood. I can't imagine why I didn't notice it had been shifted about from the cater-cornered position. Unless it was because of the shock . . ."

"That may well be it," Ellery said pleasantly. "And you, Mr. Importuna? Apparently the shift has escaped you, too."

"Mr. Importuna rarely comes down here —" Ennis began quickly.

"I can talk for myself, Peter," Nino Importuna said, and the younger man flushed again. "I did notice the desk had been moved, Mr. Queen. The moment I walked in here. But I thought the police had moved it during their first investigation." The eyes were illegible. "Does it make a difference? Do you see a meaning in it?"

"Every difference makes a difference," Ellery said. "And yes, I see a meaning in it, Mr. Importuna. Like the button and the shoeprint —"

"Button? Shoeprint?" The multimillionaire stared. "Which button? Whose shoeprint? No one has told me —"

The Inspector enlightened him with a remarkable lack of reticence. The old man's eyes were equally difficult to read.

"The button and the shoeprint were plants to incriminate your brother Marco, Mr. Impotuna," Ellery explained. "The shifting of Julio's desk appears to have had a similar motivation. Marco is left-handed. From the position of the desk when Julio's body was found — parallel to the rear wall — and judging from which side of Julio's head received the blow, could the blow have been struck by a left-handed man? Yes, it could. So again we have an indication of Marco's guilt. Or at least no incompatibility with the concept.

"But now we know that the placement of the desk was also a plant. Because what happens when the desk is returned to its usual position, to the cater-cornered position in which it actually stood when the blow was struck? In this position it would have been impossible for a left-handed blow to have been delivered to the side of Julio's head on which we find the killing wound, as the merest consideration shows. There simply isn't enough room to swing the poker and hit that side of the head. The killer must have realized this and, in order to make the supposition of a left-handed blow possible, he had to shift the desk.

"So now," Ellery said, "not only is the button suspect, not only is the shoeprint suspect, but the left-handedness is suspect, too. In short, all the evidence against Marco is suspect. Which will come as a great relief to Marco, I'm sure, but leaves us without a lead."

He looked at his father. "You knew about the desk, too."

Inspector Queen nodded. "That's why I was anxious to get you in on this, Ellery. This kind of extra-smart frame is up your alley, not ours."

"I think," Nino Importuna rasped, "I do not understand."

"Somebody not only had it in for your brother Julio, Mr. Importuna," Ellery said, "but apparently he's out to do your brother Marco dirt as well. Or at least he didn't shrink from setting Marco up for the rap, which hardly classifies him as a friend. Who hated Julio? And possibly Marco as well? Enough to murder the one and frame the other for it?"

"I already told Inspector Queen and the other police officials who've been here today, Mr. Queen, about Julio in that respect. I can't even imagine it in Julio's case. He was like a fat and frisky dog, a Saint Bernard puppy bumping into things in his play, knocking people over with his affection. He had no meanness, no wish to hurt anyone. Full of fun and jokes and good nature. Generous with money, always helping people. A pious man —"

"You're describing a saint, Mr. Importuna," Ellery murmured. "But his portrait in this apartment suggests that the saint did have a few weaknesses. Gambling, for one."

"If you're supposing that he was in financial difficulties with, say, the Mafia, or anyone in the world of violence, Mr. Queen, that would be

80

very amusing. I assure you he was not. And if Julio had been, Marco and I would have bailed him out a hundred times over." The soft lips were actually smiling.

"Women, for another," Ellery said.

"Oh, yes, women," Nino Importuna said with a shrug. "Julio had many women. By the time he was finished with them, they were richer and happier."

"Women sometimes have husbands, Mr. Importuna. Jealous ones."

"Julio didn't play around with married women," the multimillionaire said sharply. "This has always been strictly forbidden in our family. The sanctity of the marriage vows was lashed into us from childhood. Julio would have been as likely to rape a nun as bed another man's wife."

"What about your business empire, Mr. Importuna? You three could hardly have risen to where you are without having stepped on a great many toes — without, in fact, having ruined some lives. Was Julio a saint in your business affairs, too?"

The lips lifted again. "You don't hesitate to speak your mind, Mr. Queen, do you?"

"Not when murder is involved."

The multimillionaire nodded. "A dedicated man, I see. No, Mr. Queen, Julio didn't care for big business. As he often remarked, he would have been happier as a *venditore di generi alimentari,* selling *pasta* and tomatoes and cut-

81

ting cheese all day. I don't deny what you say. To make great sums of money in the international marketplace one must be — how do you say? — *inumano . . . spietato . . .* without feeling. Marco and I, mostly I, have been *spietato* when it was necessary. I never asked Julio to join us in such things, and he would have said no if I asked. I kept him clean for the sake of his peace of mind — for the sake of his soul, he'd say, laughing. As I said, a pious, a good, man. Everyone, everyone loved him."

"Not everyone, I'm afraid," Ellery said. "We know of at least one dissenter. And Marco, Mr. Importuna? Does everyone love Marco, too?"

The massive head shook, whether negatively or in irritation at the question Ellery could not decide. He said something softly and rapidly in Italian that Ellery could not catch. Observing Importuna's extraordinary eyes, he thought that perhaps it was just as well.

"I think," Inspector Queen remarked suddenly, "we'll mosey on over across the hall, Mr. Importuna, and have ourselves an overdue session with your brother Marco."

If his surroundings bespoke the man, Ellery ruminated en route, Marco Importunato was the mad sophisticate of the three brothers. His apartment was as unlike Julio's as the era of Andy Warhol differed from Michelangelo's Florence. Every ornamental sign of the late Victorian had been removed, rebuilt, or concealed.

They passed through stark white cubical rooms, like stripped hospital wards, except for the floors, which met the feet with assaults of raw and clashing colors. The occasional expected artifact of the unexpected smote the eye — a writhing piece of furniture in an improbable material; an isolated assembly of articulated junkyard sculpture; or, as on one of the walls, a gigantic Texaco pump leaning out into the room like the Tower of Pisa, about to topple onto the pop art–lover's head. In one small room Ellery paused to admire a triumph of modernity over camp, a faithful reproduction of Whistler's *Arrangement in Grey and Black* — faithful, that is, except that the old lady's hand grasped a rather heroic banana. Another room was apparently given over to psychedelic performances of light; Ellery saw equipment — floods, spots, wheels, pinpoint lights that could be played on an organ-like instrument — that must have required enough wiring for 10,000 watts. It struck him that Marco was the type of *Playboy* New Yorker who rushes out to buy a Maserati Ghibli because he is impressed with its capability to accelerate from zero to 100 mph in 19.8 seconds and heads straight for the West Side highway during the evening rush hour to try it out.

They found the owner of all these contemporary riches in an orthodox combined gymnasium and game room adjoining his private quarters. He was dressed in puce gym tights and he was sitting cross-legged on a trampoline clutching a highball glass of what looked and smelled like straight sour-mash whisky. The ebony-and-lucite bar nearby, evidently dragged in from elsewhere, showed ring traces of numerous antecedent libations.

"Nino." He crawled off the trampoline balancing the glass. "Thank God. Do you know I've been trying and trying to reach you? I've called Virginia I don't know how many times. Where have you been? My God, Nino, if ever I needed you it's been today. Most awful day of my life." Marco Importunato stumbled into his brother's arms, slopping whisky over both of them.

He began quite frankly to sob.

"Peter," Importuna said. As usual, there was nothing to be told from his tone, not annoyance or embarrassment or distaste, not even concern.

Ennis hurried forward. Between them they hauled Marco backward to a chair, Importuna taking the glass from him. Ennis grabbed a bar towel and began to dab at Importuna's jacket.

"Never mind," the multimillionaire said. "He's drunk, as you can see, Inspector Queen. I think you'd better question him another time."

"No, sir, I'll question him now, if you don't mind," the Inspector said. He stooped over the weeping man. "Mr. Importunato, do you remember me from this afternoon?"

Importunato grunted.

"Do you know who I am?"

"Sure I know who you are," Marco said with peevish clarity. "What kind of a question is that?

Anyway? You're a cop. Inspector somebody."

"Queen. This is Ellery Queen, my son. I'm sorry we've had to keep you waiting all day —"

"Damn right. Right, Nino? That's why I'm sloshed. Waiting for their damn questions and nothing to think about but poor old Julio. That poor slob. Never hurt a fly. Gimme my glass back."

His brother said, "No more, Marco."

Marco staggered upright and lunged for it. Importuna stepped in his way. The younger man clung to him, weeping again.

"What do you expect to get out of him in this condition?" Importuna said to the Inspector.

The Inspector said, "You never know. And I can't wait for him to sober up."

"But what can he know about Julio's death?"

"I don't know, Mr. Importuna. That's what I have to find out."

Ellery was taking the opportunity to evaluate the man in the gym tights. Where Nino was squat and powerful, and Julio had been large and soft, the middle brother was slight, weak boned, almost phthisical. His olive skin had a bleached look, as if it had been too long deprived of sun. There were deep anxiety lines around his mouth and bloodshot eyes.

Marco Importunato was evidently a neurotic, with a dependency on his eldest brother that must reach into many areas of his existence. Observing the sallow, sunken face lacerated with grief and fear, yet relieved at his brother's proximity, Ellery caught himself thinking of a terrified child wrapping his legs about his father. Instant analysis it might be, and consequently suspect, but it was after all the universality of such relationships that made them trite. The next moment he was not so sure. He glanced from clutched to clutched and thought he detected on the older, heavier face the faintest expression of affectionate contempt. And that would follow, too. Nino Importuna did not seem to him the sort of man who could respect a weakness, especially in one of his own blood. It struck too close to home.

Importuna signaled Ennis, and the secretary sprang forward again to help deposit Marco in the chair. The squat man went behind the bar, poured out most of the contents of the highball glass, and brought his brother the little that remained. Marco took a shaky swallow. Then he nodded at something Importuna said to him in an undertone.

"He can talk now," the multimillionaire said, and he took the glass away.

"Mr. Importunato," Inspector Queen said immediately, "do you recall early today being shown a gold button with an anchor-and-rope design and the monogram *MI* on it?"

Marco muttered something about button, button?

"Assistant Chief Inspector Mackey of Manhattan North showed it to you, Mr. Importunato, and you identified it at that time as

86

your property. Don't you remember that?"

"Oh. Sure. Sure thing. Came off a yachting jacket of mine. 'Swhat I told him, all right. Nice old bird. Terrible case of bad breath, though. His best friend ought to tell him."

"Marco," the elder brother said.

"Sì. Sì bene, Nino."

"Do you know where your button was found?"

Marco's head wobbled.

"It was found on the floor of your brother Julio's library."

"You don't say."

"Can you explain how it got there, Mr. Importunato? And when?"

Marco Importunato blinked through the fog.

Inspector Queen went to the trampoline, pulled it over near the chair, and sat down. He tapped the half-naked man's hairy knee in a friendly way. "I'm going to break one of the rules of police interrogation, Marco — you don't mind if I call you Marco? — and tell you just what else we've found out about that gold button of yours. Are you paying attention, Marco?"

"*Sì,* I mean yes."

"At first we thought that you were the man who'd had the battle with Julio, and that in the scrap he yanked the button off your jacket."

"Uhn-uhn," Marco said with an almost vigorous shake of his head.

"But on closer examination we saw that the button hadn't been pulled off your jacket, it was snipped off, most likely by a scissors. So we decided somebody's tried to frame you for the murder of your brother. Do you understand me, Marco?"

"Sure I understand you," Marco replied with dignity "And you know what I say to you? Ri . . . dic . . . u . . . lous!"

"What do you mean?"

"I can tell you who cut that button off my coat."

"You can? Who?"

"Me."

"*You?*"

"Cut it off, snip-snip, and that's it. With my bathroom scissors. Was hanging loose and I didn't want to lose it. Gold, after all. The Importunatos were ever a thrifty clan. Not that the *famiglia* had a choice. Can't be a swinger without something to swing with, hey, Nino?" Marco leered at his brother.

Importuna did not smile back.

"When did this happen, Mr. Importunato?" Ellery asked. "When did you cut the button off your jacket?"

"I don't know. What's today? Yesterday. That's it. Didn't get a chance to tell Tebaldo to sew it back on."

"Tebaldo?"

"His valet," Importuna said.

"What did you do with the button, Mr. Importunato?"

"What did I do with it?" the man in the tights said, offended. "I put it in my pocket, that's what

I did with it. Say, who are you again?"

"My name is Queen. The pocket of what? Your yachting jacket?"

"Aye, aye, sir. *Sì, capitano mio.*"

"Dad, is the jacket downtown? I assume the tech men took it."

"It's at the lab."

"I should have thought to examine it while we were down there. Mr. Importuna, where's a phone I can use?"

"There's an extension in my brother's bedroom."

"May I, Mr. Importunato?"

"Call Tokyo. Call anyplace." Marco waved amiably.

Ellery was back in a few minutes. He was pulling his nose as if it were taffy. "This one's simply overflowing with surprises, dad. I've just been informed that an examination of the left pocket — the jacket has patch pockets — shows some of the stitching's crept out, so there's a gap, not very noticeable, at the base of the pocket. It's wide enough, I'm told, for the button to have slipped through."

The Queens eyed each other.

"That *stupido* Tebaldo," Marco said, shaking his head. "I shoulda fired him the day I hired him. Hey, did you hear that? I'm a poet and I don't know it."

"Tell me something, Marco," Inspector Queen said. "You know that shoe of yours we borrowed today? The one with the crepe sole?"

"Keep it," Marco said grandly. "You can have the other one, too. I've got more shoes than Macy's and Gimbel's put together."

"Do you know there's a deep gash almost half the length of the sole?"

"What d'ye mean do I know? Course I know! Happened — when was it? Well, it isn't important. Few days ago."

"Oh?" The Inspector looked puzzled. "Happened how?"

"I was taking a special girl friend o' mine sailing in Larchmont — keep one of my boats there. She was coming in from upstate and I was at Grand Central to meet her. What do I do but step on a gobboon of chewing gum some slob 'd spit on the floor. Made me madder 'n hell. So I went downstairs to the men's room and I took the shoe off and borrowed a knife from the attendant, and while I was digging the gum out from the ripples the blade slipped and, zippo! — sweetest little gash you ever did see. Practically surgery. Oh, you did see it. That's right."

"Why didn't you tell us before about snipping the button off your jacket and slicing into the sole of your shoe?" the Inspector growled.

"You didn't ask me," Marco said, in a huff again. "Nobody asked me. Nino, gimme another drink. I'm getting good and teed off answering all these stupid questions."

"No," his brother said.

Something in his voice made Marco blink cautiously. He decided to laugh. "Y'know Nino won't touch the hard stuff? A little *vino* once in a while and that's it with him. That's my brother. Nobody'll ever catch *him* crocked. Too smart. Hey, Nino?"

"I think," Importuna said to the Inspector, "my brother's answered enough questions."

"I'm almost through, Mr. Importuna."

"I don't want to seem uncooperative, but if you're going to keep this up, I'll have to demand that one of our attorneys be present. I should have insisted on it from the start. You can see Marco's condition, Inspector. This has been a very bad day for us all —"

"What about my condition?" Marco cried. "What's wrong with my condition?" He tottered to his feet and began to wave his bony fists. "Next thing they'll be calling me a drunk. Why, I'll take any old test they wanna throw at me . . ."

Importuna nodded curtly, and Peter Ennis jumped forward once more to help him with the now bellicose man. While they were cajoling him and easing him back to the chair, the Queens took the opportunity to commune out of earshot.

"With Marco himself snipping that button off," Inspector Queen muttered, "and slicing into his shoe accidentally, there goes the frame-up theory, Ellery. The button simply fell out of that hole in his pocket, and the shoeprint in the cigar ash showing the cut is a legitimate clue. With these admissions of his, they both place Marco in that library of Julio's for real."

"With every cock-eyed thing that's happened

so far, is it all right with you if I wonder?" Ellery had transferred his yanking and hauling from nose to lower lip. "Look, dad, there seem to be ifs all over this case. Let's try to clear some of them up. Do you want to tackle Marco, or shall I?"

"I'd better do it. Importuna's set to throw his weight around. It's harder for him to give me the heave. . . . Feeling a little feisty, Mr. Impotunato? I don't think — the way things look for you right now — you can afford it."

Marco twitched. The sallow skin was beginning to show a greenish undertinge.

"Take it easy, Marco," his brother said. "Just what do you mean, Inspector Queen?"

"It's very simple. We know now that Marco was *not* framed; he's knocked that theory out by his admissions here. But we did find his button and shoeprint in Julio's library. In my book that places your brother Marco on the scene of the crime legitimately. So before the district attorney gets into the act, if Marco has an explanation I'd strongly advise him to give it."

"He does not have to tell you anything," the multimillionaire said harshly. "In fact, I'm growing very tired of this —"

"Nino." Marco Importunato raised his head from his trembling hands. "I think I'd better."

"I'd rather you kept quiet. At least until I can get Emerson Lundy up here."

"Why should I yell for a lawyer, Nino?" Of a sudden he was hysterically sober. "As if I were guilty? I have nothing on my conscience! If these people think I could kill Julio . . . My God, Julio was *famiglia* . . . blood brother. It's true, Inspector Queen, that I was in Julio's library last night. And we did have a quarrel. But —"

"What time was this, Mr. Importunato?" the Inspector asked casually, as if Marco had said something trivial.

"I don't know exactly. It was before 9 o'clock, because I do know it wasn't quite 9 when I left him." The man's blood-streaked eyes sought the Inspector's. "Left him," he said. "Alive and well."

"What about the condition of the room? The broken furniture, the knocked-over lamps —"

"I don't know a thing about that. When I walked out of Julio's library everything was in place. We didn't have a fist fight, for the love of Christ! It was just an argument, Inspector. Some hot talk between brothers. Julio and I argued a lot. Ask Nino. Ask anybody."

"Marco, I want you to keep your mouth shut," his brother said. "I order you! Do you hear me?"

"No," Marco said hoarsely. "They think I killed Julio. I've got to convince them I didn't. Ask me more questions, Inspector! Go ahead, ask me."

"About what was this particular argument last night?"

"Business. We've always had a family rule that all important investment decisions of Importuna Industries have to have the unanimous agree-

93

ment of Nino, Julio, and myself. If one of us says no, it's no deal. We don't usually have trouble agreeing. But recently Nino proposed that we set up a new corporation and buy 19,000,000 acres of Canadian Arctic land — our top geologist thinks there's a good chance that particular area is one big oil deposit — no, Nino, I'm not going to shut up! — a bigger field than Texas and Oklahoma. And we could buy it for $1.50 an acre, so the investment isn't very big. After checking the reports I agreed with Nino it was a good gamble. But Julio wouldn't go along. So we didn't have the necessary three-man agreement and we had to drop the deal. Nino was put out about it, and so was I. But — murder?" His head kept wobbling like an infant's or a very old man's. Whether it was a conscious expression of negation or simply a weakness of the neck muscles brought on by the sour-mash whisky he had consumed they could not tell.

"All right," Inspector Queen said. "So you dropped into Julio's apartment last night and you and Julio had a fight about his turndown of the deal?"

"Not a fight! An argument. There's a difference, you know!"

"I'm sorry, an argument. Go ahead, Mr. Importunato."

"I thought maybe he's in a different mood tonight, maybe I can change his mind. But no, he was still dead set against it — he'd got it into his head that either somebody'd bribed our geologist to con us out of a bundle or that, even if oil was found, it would be an economic disaster trying to handle a production and pipeline setup across thousands of miles of frozen wasteland. Anyway, one word led to another, and we wound up yelling Italian curses at each other." Marco raised his tear-swollen face. "But Julio could never stay mad very long. All of a sudden he said, 'Look, *fratello,* what are we arguing for? The hell with it, so we'll blow 28, 29 million bucks. What's money?' and he laughed, so I laughed, and we shook hands across the desk, and I said good night and walked out. And that was it, Inspector Queen. I swear."

He was sweating heavily now.

"You mean Julio gave his consent to the deal, Marco?" Nino Importuna demanded. "You didn't tell me."

"I didn't get the chance."

"Just a minute, Mr. Importuna," the Inspector said. "You didn't come to blows, Mr. Importunato? Throw things? Break anything?"

"Julio and me? Never!"

"Mr. Importunato," Ellery said; his father gave him a look and stepped back at once. "Did either you or your brother accidentally knock his ashtray off the desk?"

At this assault from another quarter Marco's head snapped about. He immediately drew it in, turtle-fashion. "I don't remember anything like that."

"When you left him, where exactly was Julio? I

95

mean, where in the library."

"I left him sitting behind his desk."

"And the desk was in its usual position? Cater-cornered?"

"That's right."

"While you were in the room, did either you or your brother move the desk?"

"Move it? Why should we move it? I don't think I even put my hand on it. And Julio never once got up from behind it."

"And you left the library no later than 9 o'clock, you said. You seemed very sure of the time, Mr. Importunato. How come?"

Marco began to shout. "Holy Mother, don't you people take a man's word for anything? A chick was meeting me at my apartment at 9:15 to go swinging. I checked my watch as I was leaving Julio. I saw it was a couple minutes to 9. That gave me just time enough to change my clothes. Satisfied?" He thrust his lower lip forward.

"Change which clothes? What were you wearing when you visited Julio last night?"

The lips clamped down. His hands were gripping the arms of the chair and his knuckles were yellow-white.

"Your yachting jacket, Mr. Importunato?" Ellery said. "The crepe-soled shoes?"

"I'm not answering any more questions. You're through here, Mister whoever-the-hell-you-are. Get out of my apartment!"

"Oh?" Ellery said. "Why the sudden clam-up?"

"Because! I can see you've made up your minds I'm guilty. I ought to've taken Nino's advice and not opened my yap. Anything else you want to find out, you can goddam well talk to my lawyer!"

Marco Importunato got to his feet and staggered over to the bar. His brother stepped in his way, and he brushed the older man violently aside, seized the whisky bottle, threw his head back, and began to glug. Importuna and Ennis closed in on him.

Under cover of the ensuing scuffle the Inspector, *sotto,* said, "What do you think, Ellery? The button could have fallen out of his pocket without his knowing. And the ashtray could have been shoved off the desk and Marco's foot stepped on the ashes."

"But the moving of the desk, dad. With Marco the killer it makes no sense. Suppose he's lying and he did move it. Why? Well, its effect is to make the murder appear as if it could have been committed by a left-handed man. And Marco's left-handed. So was he trying to implicate himself?" Ellery shook his head. "I feel like a yoyo. At the moment I'm inclined to believe him. Somebody else moved that desk. Unless . . ."

He stopped.

"Unless what, son?"

"I see," Ellery said. "That is, I think I see. . . . It's certainly a possibility."

"*What* is?"

"Dad, let's go back to Julio's library. And call

for a man to meet us there on the double with a dusting kit."

Nino Importuna and Peter Ennis rejoined the Queens in the dead man's library not long after. They had remained behind in Marco's apartment to quiet him. The Inspector was resting in an easy chair; he looked tired. Ellery stood at the desk.

"We finally got him into bed." Ennis was evidently ruffled; he was brushing his clothes with unnecessarily powerful strokes. "I sincerely hope he stays there! Marco's a bit of a handful when he's loaded."

"Tebaldo will take care of him," the multimillionaire said brusquely. "Mr. Queen, is there an end to this day? I'm beginning to feel persecuted. What is it now?"

"This business of the desk, Mr. Importuna." Ellery was staring at it; it was as they had left it, in the cater-cornered position. "With the desk cater-cornered, and on the assumption that Julio was sitting up in the swivel chair behind it facing his assailant, it wouldn't have been possible for whoever killed him, as I pointed out earlier, to have delivered a left-handed blow to the side of Julio's head where the wound is. Unless the killer struck a backhand blow, which is theoretically possible, I suppose, but I strongly question whether anyone outside a Mr. America contest could have used that poker backhandedly with sufficient force and certainly with such deadly aim as to have left that very deep and fatal wound — especially in view of the fact that the attack consisted of a single blow. No, we have to conclude that if Marco, say, had been at the striking end of the poker the wound would have been found on the opposite side of Julio's head from where it actually landed. Unless" — and Ellery swung about suddenly — *"unless our assumption is wrong and Julio was* not *facing his assailant at the instant of impact."*

"I don't see —" Importuna began.

"Hold it!" the Inspector yawped. "How exactly do you figure that, son?"

"Suppose Julio — while facing the other man in the natural vis-à-vis position — anticipated the blow. A split second before the poker came down, suppose he tried to dodge and succeeded only in swiveling his chair 180°. *So that when the blow landed he was turned completely about, facing the corner, with the* back *of his head presented to the descending poker, instead of the front, as we've been assuming.* Then the poker *would* have struck the opposite side of his head!" Ellery was striding irritably about. "Where the devil is that finger-print man?"

"I'll be damned," his father breathed; and he repeated it. Then he shook his head. "And none of us saw it! But Ellery, why a fingerprint man?"

"To test a theory that grows out of the point I just made. As the chair swiveled around with Julio trying to escape the poker, isn't it likely that he'd have thrown his arms forward instinctively to keep from toppling from the chair? And, if that happened, I don't see how Julio's hands could have avoided making contact with those walls that meet in the corner." Ellery squeezed behind the desk. "Just about here, I'd estimate — Ah, here he is! Over here, please — Maglie, isn't it?"

"But we dusted everything, Mr. Queen." The tech man was tieless, unshaven, and he was wearing a badly creased and grimy white shirt. His long face said he had been summoned from before his TV set and a bottle of beer. "What's the problem, Inspector Queen?"

The old man waved a dragging hand. "In that corner, Maglie. On the walls, Ellery'll show you."

And several minutes later they were staring at two large, smudged palm prints, shoulder high to a seated man, each print about a foot from where the two walls met, and each tilted at the finger ends toward the other.

Nobody said a word until the fingerprint man packed up and left.

"Good as a photo," the Inspector said; he had perked up considerably, and he was trying, not altogether successfully, to keep a chortle out of his voice. "That's what happened, all right! With Julio's back to the killer, the head wound is just where it would be if the strike had come from the killer's left side. No ifs about it, Julio *was* killed by a left-handed man — not just possibly any-more, but positively. That, Mr. Importuna, I'm sorry to say, along with the gold button and the shoeprint, points to your brother Marco again, only this time a lot stronger than before."

"Wait, wait," Nino Importuna said thickly. "You don't answer important questions. Why wasn't Julio left that way — I mean the way he died, facing the corner? Why was his body turned around so that his face fell forward on the desk?"

"If you weren't so upset, Mr. Importuna," Ellery said, "you'd be able to answer that yourself. We're hypothesizing now that, by the weight of the evidence, your brother Marco was Julio's murderer. Marco's just struck the lethal blow and he's looking down at Julio's unexpectedly reversed head, crushed in on the side that unmistakably betrays a left-hand blow. And he, Marco, is left-handed. Murderers don't want to be caught, Mr. Importuna, at least not consciously. So Marco turns Julio's body around to face him. In the face-to-face position, as indeed we've been assuming until now, a left-hand blow appears impossible. Isn't that reason enough for Marco not to have left Julio to be found in the about-face position?"

"Yes, but then why would Marco move the desk?" Importuna argued. "If he had left it cater-cornered, but turned Julio around to the face-to-face position so that the blow would seem to have come from the opposite side, you'd have had to say: The killer was right-handed, not left-handed. If Marco killed Julio, he had every reason *not* to move the desk. So again I ask: Why did he move it and defeat his own purpose, Mr. Queen? You can't have it both ways!"

"You know, Ellery," the Inspector said, looking tired again, "he has a point there."

Ellery was back at his nose-pulling exercise, and he was muttering, something he rarely did. "Yes . . . that's so, isn't it? If Marco was clear-headed enough to turn the body, he should have been clear-headed enough not to shift the desk. This *is* the queerest case. . . . We'd better talk to Marco again. Maybe he can clear the point up."

But they were not to talk to Marco Impotunato again on that night, or indeed on any night short of the resurrection. They found him in the tall-ceilinged gymnasium hanging halfway down the climbing rope. He had fashioned a loop in the thick hemp, thrust his head into it, evidently shinnied with it to the ceiling, and then launched himself head first toward the floor. At the end of the dive the contention of gravity with the rope claimed his neck.

That sometime imperfect gentleman's gentleman, Tebaldo, was stretched out on the trampoline like a martyr of the Inquisition, snoring with vigor and nuzzling a three-quarter-empty bottle of Italian barley brandy. Much later, on being resuscitated and approximately sobered, Tebaldo stated that his *cugino* Marco — he said he was a fifth cousin Marco had brought over from the old country at great expense in the spirit of *famiglia,* a virtue rarely to be found, alas, in this otherwise great America — had suddenly crawled forth from the bed and challenged him, Tebaldo, to a drinking competition, during which Tebaldo had attempted manfully to keep up, and about the outcome of which he, Tebaldo, remembered nothing but Cousin Marco's inflamed eyes, which he insisted — crossing himself several times — had resembled nothing so much as two of the fires of hell.

"Son, son," Inspector Queen was saying as they watched Marco's body being taken down — the lab men were confiscating most of the climbing rope, including the noose, for later examination — "anybody can get fouled up in a case like this. Don't feel so bad. I'm as responsible as you are when you get down to it. I couldn't believe all that evidence pointing straight to Marco, either. Yet it was pretty much open and shut from the start. Everything says it was Marco — the button dropped out of his pocket, the shoeprint in the ashes, that left-handed business, and now he commits suicide. Hanging himself is as good as a signed confession. . . . What's the matter, Ellery? Why the long puss again? You still aren't satisfied?"

"Since you're putting the direct question, I'll have to answer you in kind," Ellery said. "No."

"No? Why not? What's eating you now?"

"A number of things. For one, why Marco didn't leave the desk cater-cornered. For another, the fact that his committing suicide doesn't necessarily add up to a confession of murder, tempting as it is to think it does. Hanging himself might well have been the result of pouring that appalling quantity of alcohol into his system — and we saw how jittery and upset he was to start with — so much, in fact, that he may have gone temporarily psycho. In which condition a rope around his neck could seem the logical answer to his grief and guilt feelings about having quarreled with Julio. Not to mention — if he was innocent — panic over being framed.

"Also," Ellery went on, "lest we forget, dad, *cui bono?* as a canny old gent named Cicero put it some time ago. For whose benefit? Who profits by the Importunato brothers' deaths?"

"You know what I think?" the Inspector exploded. "I think you're looking for any excuse not to get back to that book of yours! All right, we'll go ask Importuna."

"Let me do the talking, dad."

The old man shrugged.

He had sent Importuna and Ennis into Marco's bedroom while the technicians worked. They found the secretary drooping in a chair, but Importuna was standing like statuary at the foot of his brother's bed, a yard away from it; Ellery received the ludicrous impression that he might be perched on one leg, like a stork or a Far East religious fanatic. Otherwise, if the multimillionaire felt anything at the violent loss of his second brother in 24 hours, Ellery was unable to detect a sign of it. Those heavy features were modeled, beyond alteration, in bronze.

"Why don't you sit down. Mr. Importuna?" Ellery asked. Distant as the man was, it was hard not to feel compassion for him. "We're not insensitive to what this must mean to you."

But Nino Importuna said, not stirring a muscle, "What do you want?" with great harshness. The espresso-colored eyes, the bitter eyes of the enemy, turned full on Ellery. Their expression, and his tone of voice, testified that something had sprung up between them, something frigid and deadly that bridged the gap and now held them fast to each other. Perhaps, Ellery thought, it's been there all the time. Perhaps he recognized me as the adversary from the the beginning.

"Who inherits your brother Julio's estate, Mr. Importuna? And Marco's? Since neither of them was married."

"No one."

"No one?"

"The conglomerate."

"Of which you're now sole owner?"

"Of course. I'm the last of the brothers. The last of our entire family."

"I thought Tebaldo is a fifth cousin."

"An old joke of Marco's that by now Tebaldo half believes. On a visit to Italy Marco got Tebaldo's sister pregnant. That was years ago. Marco hired Tebaldo as his valet to shut him up, at the same time that he made a settlement with the girl. The drunken fool isn't of our blood. So if you're asking who gains by the deaths of Julio and Marco, Mr. Queen," Nino Importuna said, "the answer is that I do. No one else."

Their eyes locked.

"Dad," Ellery said, without looking at the Inspector, "at what time last night did you say Dr. Prouty thought Julio had died?"

"Around 10 o'clock, give or take a half hour. From the way he talked, I don't think the M.E. thinks he'll be able to narrow it down any finer."

"Mr. Importuna," Ellery asked politely, "would you tell us — if you don't mind waiving your right to be silent, of course — just where you were last night between 9:30 and 10:30?"

The evenness of his voice in contrast to Importuna's harshness gave Ellery an advantage that the multimillionaire was quick to sense. When he spoke again, it was in an equally quiet tone.

"Peter."

Ennis had long since climbed to his feet, alerted by the sounds of battle under the exchange.

"Telephone upstairs and ask Mrs. Importuna to join us here right away. In view of the trend of the questioning, gentlemen, you won't mind if I call my wife in on this." He might have been referring to a trivial tidbit of gossip overheard at one of his clubs.

In no more than three minutes a chalky Tebaldo announced her arrival and rather

106

waveringly vanished.

Virginia Whyte Importuna went directly to her husband and took her place by his side. Ellery noticed with sharp interest that she did not grope for his hand, or brush against him, or allow any part of her body to come in contact with his. She simply stood near, erect and attentive, like a soldier summoned into the commanding officer's presence, an invisible gulf between them. Apparently she did not want for herself, or feel the need to give him, a physical reassurance. Or was it something else?

She was a natural very-light-café-au-lait blond with intelligent violet-blue eyes of great size, high northern European cheekbones, and a little straight nose passionately flared. Really exquisite, Ellery thought. Her beauty had an ethereal patina, almost a poetry, but he was sure that it covered a rustproof undercoating resistant to assault. What other kind of woman could cope with a man like Nino Importuna?

She wore a high-fashion dress of deceiving simplicity that set off her long legs and hourglass figure. She stood taller than her husband, even though he wore built-up shoes and she was in low heels, no doubt at his direction. Ellery judged her to be in her mid-20s. She could have passed for Importuna's granddaughter.

"Virginia, this is Inspector Queen of police headquarters, and this is Inspector Queen's son, Ellery Queen. Mr. Queen is an amateur criminologist who's interested himself in our troubles. Oh, by the way, my dear, there's been no opportunity to notify you. Marco just committed suicide."

"Marco . . . ?" Faintly. But that was all she said. She bounced back from her husband's savage announcement with the speed of a rebound. Her only concession to shock was to sink into the nearest so-called chair, in the new pneumatic mode, a billowing transparent bladder-like creation inflated with air.

Importuna seemed proud of her fortitude. He moved toward her with a fond, bitter look.

"And now it seems," he went on, "Mr. Queen's nose is sniffing in my direction. He just asked me, Virginia, where I was last night between 9:30 and 10:30. Will you tell him?"

Virginia Importuna said immediately, "My husband and I, with four guests, were at the opera." Her very feminine voice was deadly in its control, a musical enigma. Ellery was enthralled. He had heard of Importuna's devotion to his wife; he was beginning to understand why. She was the fitting lady to his lordship.

"In our season box, Mr. Queen," Importuna said. "*Parsifal.* This will shock you, no doubt, but I find *Parsifal* an interminable bore. Hard for an Italian peasant who enjoys Puccini and Rossini to sit through. But then Wagner has never been one of my enthusiasms, even ideologically, in spite of Mussolini's love for the Germans. Although Virginia adores Wagner — don't you, my dear? — naturally, being all woman. Nevertheless, I deserve a hero's medal — I endured the entire performance. Didn't I, my dear?"

"Yes, Nino."

"So that at 10 o'clock, since that's the hour you're interested in, Mr. Queen, at 10 o'clock, give or take not a half hour but more like two hours, Mrs. Importuna and I were in the company of four other people. Constantly. None of us left the box except at intermissions, and then we left as a group. Isn't that so, Virginia?"

"Yes, Nino."

"You'll want to know their names, of course. Senator and Mrs. Henry L. Factor — that's United States Senator Factor, Mr. Queen. Oh, and Bishop Tumelty of the New York diocese and Rabbi Winkleman of the Park Avenue Reformed Temple. I think the rabbi enjoyed the *Parsifal* as much as the bishop! Didn't you think so, too, my dear? Your father can, and I'm sure will, Mr. Queen, check up on our alibi with the senator and the two clergymen. Have I answered your question?"

"You've answered my question," Ellery said.

"Is there anything else you'd like to ask me?"

"A great many things, Mr. Importuna, but I have the feeling I'd be wasting your time and mine."

The squat man shrugged. "You, Inspector Queen?"

"No, sir."

But Importuna persisted in a brittle, courteous way. "Perhaps you have a few questions for my wife, Inspector, now that she's here."

"No," the old man said. "No more questions tonight."

"Benone! Allora rivederla." He clucked at his wife and Ennis as if they were small children. *"Andiamo, andiamo!* We still have work tonight, Peter, on that Midwest dairy combine. And I can't keep Mr. E waiting upstairs forever."

The Queens stood silently by as the Impotunas swept archward followed at some distance with lowered eyes by Peter Ennis. The survivor of the brothers halted so unexpectedly that his wife passed entirely under the arch and out of their view, and Ennis almost ran him down.

"Oh, Mr. Queen, it occurs to me . . ."

"Yes?" Ellery said.

"By the way, may I call you by your Christian name?"

Ellery smiled. "You mean like, say, Peter?" He saw the neckline under Ennis's dark blond hair redden, and he said, "No offense, Mr. Ennis, I was merely exemplifying a relationship."

"Touché, Mr. Queen." Importuna smiled back; his teeth were very large and disconcerting. "Are you available for profitable employment? As an executive, of course. In a confidential capacity. I can use a man of your talents and temperament."

"Thanks for the compliment, Mr. Importuna, but no, thanks. I'm the self-employed type."

"Ah. Well. Too bad. If you should ever change

your mind, Mr. Queen, you know where I am."

"I wonder," Ellery said on the way home in the squad car.

"Wha'?" Inspector Queen was nodding.

"Importuna's parting shot. About knowing where he is. I wonder if anyone, including his wife, knows where Nino Importuna is. Where he is or what he is. A tough man. Dangerous man! Talking about his wife, dad, did you notice something remarkable about Peter Ennis?"

"You hop around like hot fat," the Inspector complained. "If we're talking about Mrs. Importuna — quite a knockout, by the way — why should I notice anything about Ennis? He hardly glanced at her all the time she was there."

"To borrow from the old master, that's what's remarkable, dad. I suppose Ennis could be gay, although I don't think so, but if he's a red-blooded man how could he be in the same room with that ravishing female and not keep looking at her, reacting to her in some way?"

"You figure it out," the old man mumbled. "Far as I'm concerned the murder of Julio Importunato was solved when his brother Marco hanged himself. And, son."

"Yes, dad?"

"Don't tangle with Importuna. Take my advice, you'll only come to grief. He carries too much clout for you. . . . What? What did you say?"

"Mr. E," Ellery muttered.

"Who?"

"Mr. E. Didn't you hear Importuna? He mustn't keep Mr. E waiting. I wonder who the devil Mr. E is. . . . Dad?"

But the Inspector was asleep.

SIXTH
MONTH

June, 1967

The fetus takes on a leaner appearance.
Eyelashes and eyebrows appear.
The body grows rapidly.

They were in his den. Ennis, his long torso hunched over his notebook and the pile of papers and cables, sat at the foot of the Florentine table. To his annoyance (a chronic one) he had had to drag a chair over and make room for himself. Although Ennis had his own workroom in the apartment, Importuna had never thought to make permanent provision for him in the den during these work sessions, which had taken place regularly for years. I'm a very modest confidential secretary, Ennis thought, except for my secret life with the boss's wife; a small desk for my personal use in his sanctum isn't too much to ask of one of America's richest men. It would hardly encroach on the privacy or prerogatives of His Majesty, since I'm never within these sacred walls except on his orders and sufferance. And why the hell doesn't he have that outside wall knocked out and a picture window put in so that the den gets some decent light? As well as having a new air conditioner installed; this one literally stinks, it does such a bad job on his eternal stogy smoke.

None of this showed on Ennis's face. He waited, a paragon among puppets.

Importuna was pacing. There was a frown on

his massive face that interested Ennis. It was not the familiar frown of the *padrone,* before which presidents of companies and chairmen of boards quailed. This frown was directed toward something within himself.

Suddenly Ennis thought, Can it be fear?

The great Importuna afraid of something?

He was roused by Importuna's grating voice. "What was that last, Peter?"

"A memorandum to the sales forces of the E.I.S. offices in Zurich. Noting that the rate of redemptions over sales in the mutual funds has been running around $2-million a day. This trend must be reversed at once. Quote we must avoid at all costs a loss of confidence in the funds. All personnel are to redouble their efforts to restore a positive level of sales over redemptions as quickly as possible unquote."

"Yes," Importuna said. "A note to Mrs. Importuna: 'My dear, Instruct Mrs. Longwell to have the Kashan rug in my den taken up for the summer and sent to Bazhabatyan's for cleaning and storage. I made this request two days ago and it has not yet been done.' Signed as usual."

"With great love," Ennis murmured, writing, "Nino." When he looked up from the notebook he asked, "Is something wrong, Mr. Impotuna?"

"What do you mean?"

It was fascinating to watch Importuna pace. He took 9 steps in one direction, 9 steps back.

Never more, or less, than 9 in these pacing episodes.

Did he consciously count them, or had his obsession with his lucky number become part of his automatic nervous system?

"Nothing, really. It's just that I thought you seem disturbed this morning."

"I am! I had a transatlantic call from Von Slonem before you got here. The Ploesti deal has fallen through."

"But I thought that was firm. Locked up."

"It was! I don't know how it could have happened. Without warning — *ffft!* Up in the air. And comes down in pieces. Von Slonem was almost incoherent. Something went terribly wrong at the last moment. I wonder if my luck . . . Do you realize on which day?"

"Today is Friday."

"Today is the 9th!"

"Oh," Peter Ennis said. "Yes. Well, maybe it's good luck in disguise, Mr. Importuna. Remember what your brother Julio used to say? The sweetest-tasting deals are the ones that turn sour first. Maybe the fact that the Ploesti deal fell through on the 9th is a sign that you shouldn't have gone into it in the first place."

Importuna's frown lightened. It was incredible. A man of his acumen. "You think so, Peter?"

"Who knows, Mr. Importuna? If you have faith in any system of belief . . ."

How long, O Lord?

116

They resumed working.

Importuna's 9th step away from Ennis took him to the floor-to-ceiling bookshelves on the other side of the room. Ordinarily when he reached the shelves he would turn on his heel and take the 9-step journey back. But sometimes as he dictated to Ennis he would pause to lean against a shelf in pursuit of a thought, his right hand with its four fingers raised to one of the higher shelves, his gaze directed to the Kashan rug. During one of these reflective pauses Importuna chanced to look up and about. His glance fixed on the row of books at his eye level and all thoughtfulness fled his face. It was supplanted by something very like panic.

"Peter!" he cried in a rage.

Ennis, startled, looked around. "Yes, sir?"

"Come here!"

Ennis jumped up. "What's the matter?"

"I said come here!"

"What's wrong, Mr. Importuna?"

"This shelf — these books here —" He was almost unable to articulate.

"Books? What about them? They look perfectly all right to me."

"They are *not* perfectly all right! These three — this — *this* — *this!* — they were standing on the shelf *upside down.* Weren't they? Well, weren't they!"

Ennis stammered, "If you say so, Mr. Importuna —"

"You know they were!" the tycoon thundered.

"Why didn't you let them alone? You were the one who turned them right side up again, weren't you, Peter? Weren't you?"

"If those were the ones, Mr. Importuna. Wait, I remember now. I really didn't stop to identify the titles. I saw some books standing on the shelf upside down and I naturally righted them."

"What do you mean 'naturally'? There's nothing natural about it! Why did you do it?"

"Well, because —"

"Don't you remember my specifically ordering you not to lay a finger on *any* of the books on this particular shelf?"

Ennis was extremely pale. "I'm sorry, Mr. Importuna, I forgot. Or mistook the shelf. Anyway, all I did was —"

"All you did," stormed Nino Importuna, snatching the three books from the shelf and slamming them back into place upside down, "was something you don't begin to understand! No wonder the Ploesti deal blew up. From now on, Peter, when I say don't touch something, *don't touch it*. Do you understand? Hand me the direct line to the office."

Ennis ran to the table, ignored the telephone console, snatched up the red phone, and ran back with it to Importuna.

"Get me Crabshawe . . . John! Importuna. Call a meeting of the staff. Immediately. And arrange for a trans-ocean conference call among ourselves, Bucharest, and Von Slonem. . . . I *know* the Ploesti deal fell through, John! But now

118

I also know why, and I think it can be saved. I'm going to make them a new offer I guarantee they won't turn down. . . . Yes. I'll be with you in exactly" — he glanced at his watch, and he actually smiled — "exactly 9 minutes." He hung up and Ennis took the instrument from him. "The car, Peter."

"I've already alerted McCoombes. He'll have the car out front by the time you get downstairs, Mr. Importuna. Is there anything you want me to do meanwhile?"

"No, we'll finish up here tomorrow morning. Just take care of the matters I've already noted. And tell Mrs. Importuna I'll let her know later today about this evening. I don't know how long those Rumanians will tie me up." Importuna showed his great teeth again and tapped Ennis affectionately on the chest. "I'm sorry I shouted at you, Peter. But you got me very upset."

He secmed in high humor as he strode out.

Ennis sank into Importuna's chair. His hands were shaking, and he grasped the arms of the chair to steady them. His chest itched whcre Importuna's double finger had tapped it.

Two cool, soft hands slipped over his eyes from behind.

Ennis's hands flew up to hers, trying to detach them. "Virginia, I didn't hear a sound. He may still be here —"

"He's left, darling," Mrs. Importuna said. "It's all right. I made very sure."

She came round and sat down on his lap,

twining her bare arms about his neck.

"Honey. If Editta, or Crump —"

"I sent Editta out on an errand. She'll be gone for an hour. And Crump's in the pantry with Mrs. Longwell, polishing the silver for our dinner party tonight."

"You may not have any dinner party tonight. He told me to tell you he'd let you know later today. He may be tied up buying half of Rumania. Are you sure — ?"

"Don't be so jittery," she said, breathing into his ear. "Nobody's going to catch us doing anything naughty. Or are they?"

They embraced with familiar passion in her husband's chair.

"You know something, Peter?" Virginia murmured after a while.

"What, Virginia?"

"I'd like us to make love right here."

"Here! Where?"

"On Nino's table. He's so stupid about it. Just because it belonged to a Medici. I'll bet it's seen a lot worse." She laughed and deliberately nipped his ear. "What do you say?"

"Sounds groovy. But give me a rain check, baby. I'm still a little shook up."

"Oh?" She sat up and regarded him at arm's length. "Something happened?"

"Before he left he almost bit my head off. And you'd never guess what about."

"You didn't kiss his ring."

"This isn't funny! A long time ago, he'd told

me never to touch any of the books on some shelf or other back there. Hell, I'd forgotten all about it, it seemed so childish. All the damn shelf held were ordinary books. Yesterday I had to come in here for something — Nino wasn't here — and I noticed some books on one of the shelves put in the wrong way. You know, upside down. Well, you know how compulsively neat I am. I turned them right side up without giving it another thought. Practically a reflex. And that was that — I thought. I didn't even recall that that was the taboo shelf."

"And he noticed?"

"Noticed! He went up through the ceiling. You'd think I'd committed a major crime. He turned them back upside down and practically threatened to skin me alive if I ever disobeyed an order of his again. I had all I could do to keep from laying one on that eagle beak of his, Virgin. It's getting tougher for me by the day. I don't know how much longer I can take this — sucking up to my lord and master so I can catch a glimpse or two of you once in a while!"

"My poor baby . . ."

"If it didn't mean not seeing you every day, I'd have let him have it long ago and walked out."

"Darling . . ."

"Do you suppose he's slipping his cable? Keeping books on a shelf upside down on purpose! I swear, Virgin, since Marco knocked Julio off and hanged himself, Nino's been sliding downhill fast."

"This book thing," Virginia said thoughtfully. She jumped off Ennis's lap and went over to the bookshelves, and he followed her. "It must have something to do with those crazy 9s of his, Peter."

"How could it have?"

"I don't know. But whenever he acts irrational it's somehow involved with his 9s. Are these the ones?"

"That's right."

She tilted her head, reading the titles upside down. "*The Founding of Byzantium.* Author somebody named MacLister. There's suspense reading for you . . . *The Defeat of Pompey*, A. Santini. A real thriller . . . And the third one is *The Original KKK*, by a J. J. Beauregard. Yippee."

"Wild."

"I must be wrong, Peter. These can't have anything to do with his 9s. Do you suppose there's a clue in some of these other books on the shelf? Even though they're right side up like a good book should?"

"You mean like *The Landing of the Pilgrims*, honey-bunch? Or — now here's a candidate for the bestseller list if ever I saw one: *Magna Carta at Runnymede.* A real smasheroo. And — hold your breath, baby, this one is a significant lesson for our times — *The Establishment of the Roman Empire.*"

Peter Ennis laughed. He looked around.

Then he picked up Virginia Whyte Importuna and carried her over to the Medici desk.

SEVENTH AND EIGHTH MONTHS

July and August, 1967

Maturation proceeds.

A layer of fatty matter is deposited under the skin whose function is to nourish and protect the fetus during the early part of its coming emergence into the world.

NINTH MONTH

LABOR

The redness fades from the skin. Fingernails and toenails are defined. Glandular secretions and excretions prepare the fetus for the changes soon to come.

The first rhythmic contractions signal the onset of the mother's labor.

The baby is about to be born.

Nino was charming, almost delightful, that day. In fact Virginia had to try a little not to like him. She did not find the exertion excessive; still, there it was.

It was the 9th of September, a day to commemorate, but not only or even principally because it was Nino's 68th birthday. The greater happiness of the day lay in the fact that it was also their fifth wedding anniversary. And their fifth wedding anniversary had a very special significance for Virginia Whyte Importuna (and, by secret extension, Peter Ennis). For it demarcated the time zone specified in their prenuptial agreement, the date before which Virginia Whyte had waived all property and dower rights when she should become Nino Importuna's wife, and after which — if still living with him as his wife — she became his sole heir.

The penthouse had never experienced such traffic. People dropped in throughout the day with gifts and flowers — Virginia's father; executives of Importuna's Industries' component corporations based in New York; friends from the jet set; ambassadors and other dignitaries of foreign delegations to the United Nations who found it tactically expedient to remain in Nino

Importuna's good graces, especially those representing countries in which Importuna money was invested; colleagues in the fraternity of finance; the never-absent politicos; even the clergy. Messengers deposited overflowing cartons of congratulatory telegrams and cables from Importuna's 10,001 industrial connections at home and overseas.

Virginia was warily impressed, especially since for the first time in their marriage Nino devoted himself wholly to her that day. Several times Peter Ennis reported to him that Mr. E was on the telephone pleading urgency and requesting leave to come to the penthouse, only to be told with a tooth-filled smile that all business "must wait until tomorrow. *Lavoro sempre, ma non oggi.* Today belongs to my wife." Since Mr. E to her certain knowledge had open sesame to the penthouse day and night, Virginia could scarcely believe her ears.

The callers straggled off toward the end of the afternoon and, as the dinner hour approached, the Importunas were finally alone. This was the moment Virginia had dreaded all day, in spite of the day's aura of felicity. The five-year history of their unattended husband-and-wife encounters had still not inured her to the prospect.

To her surprise he said, "You know, my dear, Peter is still at his desk — much as I'd like to have given him the day off, there were some matters that had to be taken care of. I feel a bit guilty about it, considering the occasion. Would you

126

mind very much if I asked him to join us for dinner?"

"Why, Nino, how thoughtful of you." Virginia said it at once, in her most detached tone. And how adept we've become, Peter and I, she thought, in pulling the wool over Nino's eyes. It was going to be a strain, of course; it always was when they were *à trois*. But on the other hand to be *à deux* with him was more like suffering a rupture. "Naturally I don't mind. If it would please you."

"Wouldn't it please you, Virginia?"

Why had he said that? Nino had the uncanniest way of making her feel uneasy. Nothing must go wrong now, she told herself fiercely. I've gone through too much for too long to blow it at the moment of victory.

She shrugged. "It really doesn't matter to me one way or the other."

"Then I'll ask him."

She could tell from signs only she could read (she reassured herself) that Peter, too, regarded Nino's sudden invitation as a not unadulterated sugarplum. Nevertheless, they made a civilized threesome at table. César, the chef, a Swiss who specialized in Italian cuisine, had outdone himself making Virginia's favorite dishes; the table wines were impeccable; the champagne flowed. Peter proposed a toast to her husband's birthday (how she hated herself for her hypocrisy, but it was chronic, more like a cancerous agony kept to the level of tolerance by sedation than an open wound) and another to their wedding anniversary, which amused and excited her in its reminder of what loomed ahead, although she maintained her pretense of aloofness with the competence of long practice.

Peter brought forth his gifts. For Importuna's birthday he had unearthed at some sale or other a letter from Gabriele D'Annunzio to his inamorata, Eleonora Duse. It was housed in a large lush ormolu frame embowered in laurel leaves and peeping satyrs, and it included handsome photographs of the poet-soldier and the actress. The letter was dated 1899. Importuna read it aloud to Virginia, translating into pedantic English as he went along. It expounded D'Annunzio's philosophy of passing — "the pleasures of the senses alone give meaning to life." Importuna was visibly pleased with it — "How clever of you, Peter, to find such a treasure from the year of my birth! I shall have it hung in my den immediately."

Virginia thought it rather too dangerously clever of Peter, considering its subject matter.

For their anniversary he presented them with a mid-19th century vase of *reticello* glass decorated with swans in *lattimo*. Both Virginia and Nino were fond of Venetian glass, and the penthouse was filled with specimens of the *vetro di trina* or lace glass of which Peter's vase was a relatively recent example; Importuna's collection included rare *reticello* dating back to the 15th century. The industrialist was nevertheless generous in his thanks, and Virginia echoed him with what she silently hoped was just the right degree of disengaged warmth.

Then it was her turn. She had given a great deal of thought to her gift; she had commissioned it through an agent in Italy months before. Virginia clapped her hands, and Crump came into the dining room pushing a serving cart with all the aplomb of a five-star general. He brought it to rest at Importuna's chair and sedately retreated. On the cart stood 9 large sealed flagons of exquisite crystal, each monogrammed *NI* in platinum, and each filled with what appeared to be the same colorless liquid.

"As I've had to keep telling you, Nino, you're very hard to buy gifts for," Virginia said with a smile. "So these are for the man who has everything. Happy birthday, dear, and anniversary." She managed the endearment without corrupting the smile.

Importuna was examining the flagons with quizzical interest. Suddenly his face cleared.

"Grazie, sposa," he murmured. "I see you remembered. I'm touched. *Grazie di nuovo."*

"But what is it?" Peter asked. "It looks like water."

He knew very well what it was; she had discussed her choice with him.

"It is water," Virginia said. "During our honeymoon in Rome five years ago, Nino took me to the Piazza di Spagna and showed me the Barcaccia fountain, designed by Pietro Bernini in 16-something — that's Bernini the elder, not the famous one. The water of the Barcaccia fountain, Nino told me, is supposed to have unusual qualities and a superior taste. And in fact, while we were standing there, a steady stream of people came from the nearby artists' quarter — Via Margutta and Via del Babuino — don't you love that name? Street of the Baboon? — carrying jugs and buckets and filling them from the fountain the way people had been doing, Nino said, for 350 years."

"It is superior, in spite of the Roman scoffers," Importuna said. "César will kiss me. I'll let him have some to cook with. Artichokes and zucchini cooked in this water have special *brio,* as they say. It's true. What an imaginative present, Virginia. So full of sentiment. I thank you again. Especially for humoring what I know you consider my imbecile superstition — not only bottles of water from the Barcaccia, but 9 of them! It is too much.

"And now, my dear," he said, "I have my anniversary present to you."

And plumbed his breast pocket for something.

So finally . . . finally. The climax of her day. The climax of her five years of days. And their hideous nights. Under cover of the Assisi-work tablecloth Virginia pressed her nails into her palms. Her face remained pleasantly expectant.

"I don't suppose, Virginia," her husband said as he brought out of his dinner jacket a blue-backed paper, "you've forgotten the rather special meaning of this anniversary."

"No, Nino, I haven't," she said steadily enough, although her heart was bonging against her chest.

"Five years ago you signed this paper. Under its terms you gave up any and all claims on me and my estate, even a dower right, for the full five-year period. Well, the period has passed, and you're still my wife and living with me." Importuna's glance took her in at the opposite end of the table with unconcealed pride of ownership — the exquisite northern features, the fine coloring, the gossamer quality, the depth of the womanliness half bared by her décolletage — and with a tremor, suppressed at once, she saw the dreaded fire kindle in his eyes. "A deal is a deal, Virginia. The test is passed, the trial's over, the agreement is null and void, as the lawyers say. So tear it up, my dear, burn it, keep it — it doesn't matter now. It's meaningless. Peter, will you hand this to Mrs. Importuna for her disposal?"

And he gave the blue-backed paper to Ennis, who passed it along in silence to Virginia.

"You'll understand, Nino, if I look this over?"

He waved his four-fingered hand and displayed his teeth in appreciation. "It would be very foolish, *cara*, not to. And you are not, thank the Blessed Mother, a fool. Why should you trust a man who forced a deal like this on you? Verify it, by all means."

The irony, if that was what it was, did not

deter her. "Excuse me, Peter. You don't mind, do you?"

"Of course not, Mrs. Importuna."

She deliberately examined the agreement, down to the date, the signatures, and the notary's imprint. Then she nodded, refolded the paper, and tucked it into her bosom.

"I've decided to hang on to it, Nino. As a memento. Now how about the second part of our bargain?"

Importuna chuckled. "Tell her, Peter."

"I beg your pardon?"

"The will I had you witness the other day. The new one I asked you to read."

"Oh! Mr. Importuna had a new will drawn the other day, Mrs. Importuna, by one of his personal attorneys. I was called in to witness the signature, along with two others, and Mr. Importuna asked me afterward to read it. Do you want me to tell Mrs. Importuna the substance of it, Mr. Importuna?"

"Please."

"It's a basically simple document, although for estate tax purposes and so on a rather complicated trust structure has been set up by the lawyer. In effect, though, it leaves Mr. Importuna's entire estate to you." Peter uttered a mendacious what-a-good-little-confidential-secretary-am-I cough. "Congratulations, Mrs. Importuna."

"Thank you." Virginia rose and went round to her husband and to his evident astonishment and pleasure kissed him on the forehead. "And thank you again, Nino."

"I've made you happy," Importuna murmured. "You don't know how I wish — I wish —"

He stopped with a gasp, and Virginia said sharply, "What's the matter?"

His face had gone yellow, a muddy yellow. He was doubled over in what seemed to be an attack of some sort.

Ennis jumped up. "What's wrong, Mr. Importuna?"

He waved them off. "Nothing, nothing. Indigestion — cramps. And I'm dizzy — I've had too much to drink tonight — not used to it . . ." His face had broken out in perspiration. But he tried a joke. "How often does a man celebrate a fifth wedding anniversary with a wife like mine?"

"Stop talking," Virginia said, holding a glass of water to his lips. "Here, take a swallow. Peter, you'd better ring up Dr. Mazzarini —"

"No, no, he'll complicate my life with a thousand unnecessary tests. I'll take some aspirin and a dose of milk of magnesia and go to bed, and I'll be all right in the morning. . . . The pain's already letting up." Importuna got to his feet with the aid of the back of his chair. "My dear, will you forgive me? Spoiling your anniversary this way . . ."

"Here, let me help you to your room," Ennis said, taking his arm.

"I'll manage by myself, Peter, thanks. You

keep Mrs. Importuna company — César will be crushed if his dessert is ignored. *Cara,* I'll see you at breakfast." He waved again and quickly, if unsteadily, left.

They remained where they were, almost touching. But when Peter reached for her and opened his mouth to say something, Virginia stepped back, shook her head, and put a finger to her lips.

"Well, Peter," she said in a clear voice, "shall we sit down and finish dinner? Please ring for Crump. Or isn't that he now?"

Only later, when they were safely alone, beyond the possibility of eavesdropping, did they communicate.

"Did you get the feeling that he *knows?*" Peter muttered. "Though if he does, why isn't he acting the outraged husband bit? What do you think, Virgin?"

"You have a positive gift for inventing nick-names," Virginia murmured from the depths of his arms.

"No, seriously."

"I don't know what Nino knows or what he doesn't. He's the original sphinx."

"Why did he have me read his new will the other day? Why did he ask me to dinner tonight?"

"Worrywart." Virginia laughed. "That will *is* all right, isn't it, Peter? No gimmicks or weenies?"

"No conditions at all. At his death you'll come

into ownership and control of half a billion dollars. Some people have all the luck."

"Don't we?" Virginia drew a long, long breath. "Woo-eee! But Peter."

"Yes, baby."

"We'll have to be extra careful from now on."

"Why extra?"

"Wills can be changed."

"Oh," said Peter Ennis, "Well, don't worry about it, my little chicken. I think we're over the hump."

TERM

It is born.

The next morning, quite late, as Crump held her chair in the breakfast room, Virginia Whyte Importuna asked, "Where is Mr. Importuna?"

"He hasn't appeared this morning as yet, madam, from his bedroom."

"Nino still asleep? At this hour? That's not like him."

"I presume the excitement and so on of yesterday, madam."

"It's true he didn't feel well at dinner last night and went straight to bed," Virginia said. She frowned. "Hasn't Vincenzo said anything?"

"Mr. Importuna's man has strict orders never to disturb the master, madam, until he's rung for."

"I know that! But orders are made to be broken, Crump. That's what distinguishes people from robots!"

"Yes, madam. Do you wish me to look in on Mr. Importuna?"

"I'll do it myself."

She was dressed in a billowing morning gown, and as she swept through the vast museum of her home she thought, If I had a candle in my hand I'll bet I'd be mistaken for Lady Macbeth.

Importuna's bedroom door was closed.

She tried the knob and it turned. She raised her hand, hesitated, then knocked lightly.

"Nino?"

They had had separate bedrooms since very early in their marriage, when Virginia first faced one of the bitterer truths of her bargain. You blackmailed me into marrying you, she had told him, and you're keeping me married to you by the stick and the carrot, and as your wife I have to endure your bestialities, but there is nothing in our contract that says I must occupy your bedroom after you've been slaked. I demand sleeping quarters of my own.

He had supplied them instantly. So long as you understand your duties, *sposa*, he had said with a mock bow of his squat — to her, grotesque — figure.

"Nino?" Virginia knocked again.

And yet, she thought, no physical violence, ever. Merely humiliations. Merely! Often she would have preferred the violence. To the abasement, the cruel degradation of her womanhood. As if she were in her own person responsible for his deficiency as a man and must be made to pay and suffer for it.

"Nino!"

From beyond the door still nothing.

So Virginia flung it aside and opened her mouth and was surprised that her shriek came out in a puff of silence. But she persisted, and eventually the shrieking had a sound to it. Then Crump came running as if for his stately, superior life, and Editta to add to the noise, and Vincenzo, and other servants, even the magnificent César, and at last Peter, from his workroom. Peter, who glanced for a full five stricken seconds into Importuna's bedroom. Then he reached in and grasped the handle of the door and pulled it viciously to. And grabbed the shrieker by both arms, cast her bodily at Crump, and shouted, "Do something human for once in your life, will you? Take care of Mrs. Importuna. The police — I've got to call the police."

AFTERBIRTH

The placenta is a spongy oval structure in the mother through which the fetus is nourished during pregnancy.

It is expelled immediately after the child is born.

September — October, 1967

The fantasia of the Importuna-Importunato case
(all involved in the investigation agreed that the
murder-suicide-murder sequence of the brothers' fate constituted three links in the same
chain) was, for Ellery, only beginning. Its in-
credibilities induced the kind of ratiocinative
headache he normally enjoyed looking back on
in the pain-free aftermath of success; but during
the migraine of the Importuna affair, with its
brain-cell-smashing bombardment by a verita-
ble ammo dump of number 9s, he found himself
wishing at times that he had chosen a simpler av-
ocation, like pursuing the FitzGerald-Lorentz
contraction to the infinite end of the finite universe or inventing a convincing explanation of
the Möbius strip.

The immediate facts of Nino Importuna's
murder were unpromising enough to please the
most passionate partisan of lawlessness and dis-
order. The industrialist had dined *a casa* with his
wife and confidential secretary at the conclusion
of a happy holiday, his combined 68th birthday
and fifth wedding anniversary; during dinner he
had suddenly complained of dizziness and

stomach pains, but he had shaken off a suggestion to call his physician, saying that his indisposition was not serious enough for medical treatment; he had refused assistance and retired to his private quarters under his own power after promising to take a home remedy and go to bed.

In his bedroom he had summoned his valet, Vincenzo Ricci, and told the man to get him out of his clothes and turn down his bed. He had then dismissed Ricci for the night. As Vincenzo was leaving he had seen his employer, in the bathroom, reach into the medicine chest. The valet was apparently the last person, aside from the murderer, to have seen Importuna alive. No, Mr. Importuna had not seemed very sick, merely in a little distress.

Mrs. Importuna said that she had not entered her husband's bedroom that night, or even looked in on him, for fear of awakening him. "If he were feeling worse," she told the first detectives to reach the scene, the men who were officially carrying the case, "he would either have rung for Vincenzo or called me. As I heard nothing I assumed he was asleep and feeling all right."

Peter Ennis, the secretary, had left the penthouse immediately after Mrs. Importuna and he finished their dessert, he said, and he had gone home to his bachelor pad; he occupied an apartment in a converted brownstone a few blocks west.

A small bottle of aspirin, a large bottle of milk

of magnesia with the cap off, and a tablespoon coated white with the dried antacid-laxative, were standing on the marble counter beside the washbasin in the bathroom.

The body, dressed in the silk pajamas which Vincenzo Ricci testified to having laid out for him the previous evening, was lying in the king-size bed covered by a light summer silk comforter. Only the head was exposed, what remained of it. There was a great deal of blood on the bedclothes and headboard, very little elsewhere. Unlike the case of Julio Importunato, his brother's head had been the target of repeated blows; the medical examiner counted 9 different skull fractures. Apparently Importuna had been bludgeoned to death in his sleep. There was no sign of a struggle, and nothing — according to the valet — was missing or out of place.

Importuna's wallet, containing several thousand dollars in cash and a wealth of credit cards, lay undisturbed on the night table beside his bed.

A blow had shattered his wristwatch, which was still on his wrist; in his malaise he had obviously forgotten to remove it. It was a custom-made platinum Italian-Swiss watch with rubies in place of numerals, except for the number 9 position, which was occupied by the numeral 9 instead of a ruby.

The weapon, a heavy cast-iron abstract sculpture, had been tossed onto the bloodstained bed beside the corpse. There were no fingerprints on the sculpture and no fingerprints in the bedroom except Importuna's own, the valet Ricci's, and those of a Puerto Rican housemaid who cleaned the premises as part of her chores. The killer had presumably worn protective covering on his hands.

The question of how the killer gained entrance to the building without being seen was open. The elderly night security guard, an ex-New York City policeman named Gallegher, swore up and down and sidewise that no one unknown to him had got past him. On the other hand, it was a large building, he could not have been everywhere at once, and the detectives agreed that a determined intruder could have managed, by patient observation and the seizure of an opportunity, to slip by Gallegher unseen.

To have gained entry to the penthouse apartment without leaving a trace, the detectives reasoned, the industralist's killer might have been either admitted by a confederate inside or provided with a key to the front door, which was equipped with a tamper-proof lock of special manufacture. A preliminary investigation of the household staff was begun, and a broad locksmith search was ordered on the possibility that a duplicate key had been made.

If the murder and suicide of Julio and Marco Importunato had registered on the seismographs of the world's financial centers, the murder of the head of Importuna Industries — the senior and last-surviving brother — rocked them wildly. The securities shock was felt over most of the globe — in New York, London, Paris, Antwerp, Brussels, Zurich, Berlin, Vienna, Athens, Cairo, Hong Kong, Tokyo, even in southern and eastern Africa, where Importuna capital was substantially invested. Two paperback biographies of the murdered industrialist sprouted on the racks and newsstands within three weeks of his death. National Educational Television convoked a roundtable of bankers and economists to discuss the probable long-term effects of Importuna's departure from the money marts of the world. Sunday newspaper supplements indulged in lurid, largely fanciful, detail about his beginnings, his private life, and his rocket rise into the stratosphere of industrial power.

And overnight his widow became the most written- and talked-about woman on earth, a preeminence she was to maintain for over a year, until Mrs. John F. Kennedy became Mrs. Aristotle Socrates Onassis. It was not only because of the fact that the brutal murder of her husband had made Virginia Whyte Importuna (as one female wit put it, "in nine fell swoops") one of history's wealthiest women. She was also, indisputably, one of the most photogenic. Her cheekbones caught shadows that hollowed her face into a lovely mask of tragedy, and her great light-colored eyes in some photographs gave her an unearthly look.

The mixture of unique riches and unusual

Importuna's wristwatch during the attack stopped the watch at 9 minutes past 9 o'clock. I wouldn't have believed it unless I'd seen the watch myself. And by the way, it's no accident that when Nino ordered that watch made for him he stipulated, as I'm sure he did, the use of rubies. Rubies, along with garnets and bloodstones, are considered lucky stones by people who are influenced by that sort of thing. Interestingly enough, you garner the luck when you wear the lucky gems next to your skin. Nothing can get closer to your skin than a wrist-watch."

The Inspector was not so much silent as speechless. But finally he managed to say, "And the number of blows."

"Right, 9 distinct and separate skull fractures, from 9 blows. And Doc Prouty says he had to have been dead well before the 9th blow was delivered."

"But that's all the 9s in the murder."

"That's not all the 9s in the murder, dad. The weapon, that abstraction in cast iron. With that graceful loopy curve? Didn't you notice it has the general appearance of a number 9?

"So that's three 9-elements in the murder itself," Ellery declaimed to his feet as he blundered about pulling his nose, "and I refuse to accept even the mathematical possibility that they were coincidences. Death at 9:09 P.M., caused by a weapon in the shape of a 9, a weapon moreover that struck Importuna's head 9 times

158

fanatical, illogical belief in the mysterious power of an abstraction. It was a number, the number 9, Importuna's totem, his life sign, his trademark, as the elephant had served a similar function for e.e. cummings, one erudite commentator pointed out. The late industrialist had made of the number 9 an axle about which revolved virtually every spoke of his existence.

"All right," Inspector Queen said fitfully. "I'll discuss it with you. Spout away if you have to. But don't expect me to buy it, Ellery, I'm up to here in trouble on this case. I'm not about to make a jackass of myself with this baloney about magic numbers."

"Did I use the word *magic?*" Ellery protested. "I merely said that for once the newspapers are justified, I mean in leaning on this 9 thing of Importuna's. How can you overlook it, dad? It was central to his character."

"Is it going to help nail his killer is what I'm interested in," his father grumbled. "Well, is it?"

"I don't know. It might very well, in the end."

The Inspector implored heaven with his eyebrows. "Well, go! I said I'd listen."

"Let's start at the start. Nino's start. He was born when? September 9, 1899. The 9th day of the 9th month."

"Big deal."

"And the year 1899 is a multiple of 9."

"A what?"

"The number 1899 can be divided by 9 evenly."

"So what?"

"Next: Add the digits of 1899, 1 plus 8 plus 9 plus 9, and what do you get? 27. 27 is also a multiple of 9. And if you add together the two digits of 27 — 2 and 7 — you get 9 again."

"Ellery, for heaven's sake."

"Well, don't you?"

"You can't be serious."

"Importuna was. Exactly what started him on this lifelong obsession with 9s we'll probably never dig out. Maybe it was the 9-ness of his birth date, and/or the fact that he happened to be born with 9 fingers instead of the regulation 10. Or something significant, possibly traumatic, could have happened to him on, say, his 9th birthday. Whatever it was, once it took hold it never let go of this tough, cold-blooded businessman.

"You can't overlook the strength of the grip it had on him when you realize that he went so far as to change his family name. Family and everything pertaining to it are matters of tremendous pride to the Italian *contadino*. Yet Nino dropped the last two letters out of his surname and legally became Importuna — something, I point out, his two brothers absolutely refused to do. Why Nino Importuna instead of Nino Importunato? That's not a very drastic change. It's hardly a change at all. Yet to Nino it obviously had great meaning. Why? Because it turned an 11-letter name into a name of 9 letters!

"Don't keep shaking your head, dad. It sounds silly to you, but it didn't to Importuna. There's something here, something important. I know it, I feel it. . . . Take his first name. What was it?"

"What was it? Nino!"

"Wrong. Tullio. I took the trouble to have it looked up. When he petitioned the court to allow him to change his surname from Importunato to Importuna, he petitioned at the same time to change his Christian name from Tullio to Nino. Tullio is what he was christened in the tiny church in his hometown in Italy. I cabled a private investigation agency in Rome to get the information. Tullio. Why did he have it changed to Nino?"

"Nino," the Inspector said, sucked in in spite of himself. "N-i-n-o. That's pretty close to n-i-n-e. Does Nino mean 9 in Italian? . . . What am I jabbering about!"

"No, Nino doesn't mean 9 in Italian. In Italian it means child. The word for 9 is *nove*."

"Is there an Italian Christian name that starts with N-o-v-e?"

"No, or I'm sure he would have appropriated it. So again — why Nino? Was it because it was the closest name to the look and sound of his lucky number that he could come up with? I don't believe so. In fact, I've done some boning on this, dad. You're going to think I'm mad, or drunk . . ."

"I already think so," his father said with a tired

wave. "So go ahead."

"We're never going to prove this, but I'm convinced that Tullio Importunato went into the mystique of the numeral 9 with all 9 fingers and both feet before he turned himself into Nino Importuna. There's a great deal to go into, since from antiquity 9 has been held to be one of the important mystical numbers. It can be found virtually everywhere in the ancient world.

"According to the Pythagoreans, for instance, man is 'a full chord' — 8 notes, diapason — which together with Deity becomes 9.

"It represents the 9-lettered name of God. It's 3 times 3 — 3 being the perfect number, the trinity. Lars Porsena swore by the 9 gods. There were 9 rivers of hell; in some accounts the River Styx wound around the infernal regions in 9 circles. Jesus died on the cross at the 9th hour. The early christian fathers listed 9 orders of angels. There were 9 spheres in the original Ptolemaic astronomy; that's where Milton got his 'celestial syrens' harmony that sit upon the nine enfolded spheres.' Scandinavian mythology conjured up 9 earths. Deucalion's ark, before it landed on Mount Parnassus, was buffeted about for 9 days. The Hydra had 9 heads. We meet the Nine Worthies in Shakespeare's *Love Labour's Lost* and in Dryden, 3 heroes from the Bible, 3 from the classics, and 3 from the age of chivalry — or, as Dryden puts it, 'Three Jews, three pagans, and three Christian Knights.' May I add et cetera?"

The Inspector opened his mouth but Ellery

had already plunged on.

"Folklore is chock-full of it. The abracadabra is worn for 9 day, before it's flung into a river. To see the fairy people all you have to do is put 9 grains of wheat on a four-leaf clover. And so on endlessly. To this day, we drink a toast to people of exceptional merit with a "three-times-three," and it's common practice in renting a commercial building to find that the lease extends for a term of 99 years. Heraldry recognizes 9 different crowns and 9 marks of cadency, and church architects speak of the 9 kinds of cross. If you're 'dressed to the 9s,' you're perfectly attired; and let's never forget that '9 tailors make a man.' If something is 'to the 9th degree,' it's superplus; if you have 'the 9 points of the law' on your side, you have every possible advantage short of actual right. Shall I go on?"

"Please, no," his father groaned. "Granted from all the evidence you're tossing at me, 9 is one hell of a number. But what of it, Ellery?"

"To Importuna, evidently a great deal. So much, in fact, that I'm prepared to bet he went back to the old Chaldean and Hebrew alphabets, which assigned number values to individual letters. Look up Cheiro's *Book of Numbers*. You'll find that the letter N has the value of 5, I of 1, O of 7. N-I-N-O gives you 5 plus 1 plus 5 plus 7, or a sum total of 18. 18? 18 is made up of 1 and 8. And 1 and 8 total . . . 9! Incidentally, the Hebrew word *chai* means *life* — the Jewish toast *L'Chayim* means *To Life*. The numerical designation of *chai* is 18, the first multiple of 9, and it's a number full of merit, being associated with giving and charity.

"I know it's a cockamamie, dad, but I tell you with pure, unqualified, absolute conviction that Tullio turned himself into Nino because back in the recesses of antiquity somebody worked out a symbological system whereby N-I-N-O adds up to — here we go again — 9."

Silence and the faint dropping of jaw.

Finally Inspector Queen clicked his dentures decisively. "All right, son, I'll put a down payment on it. What have I got to lose? On the other hand, what have I got to gain? How does it advance us?"

"The question is more properly, How did it advance Nino? Apparently in the proverbial leaps and bounds, judging by his fabulous success. Do you want a rundown on the extent to which he worshiped at the shrine of the great god 9? It's all in the fine print of the background reports I've been studying for the past two days, and which nobody but I seems to be taking seriously."

"What do you mean?"

"Importuna would sign contracts and other important documents only on the 9th day of the month, or the 18th which is 1 plus 8, as I just said, or the 27th, which is 2 plus 7.

"New ventures of Importuna Industries were never — repeat, never — entered into or launched, or old ventures liquidated, except on a

154

9th, an 18th, or a 27th. Even, be it noted (and to the investigator's credit he did note it) if it caused a delay that meant considerable inconvenience to the parties. Even if the delay resulted in huge gobs of money being lost — in one instance cited by the executive vice-president of one of Importuna Industries' participating companies, Importuna held up the consummation of a deal for three days until the 18th of the month, in the full knowledge that the holdup was going to cost the parent company over $20,000,000. Importuna, he said, never hesitated in ordering the delay.

"Importuna's marriage," Ellery continued. "Note that he arranged to marry Virginia Whyte on September the 9th in the year 1962. The 9th day of the 9th month in a year whose integers total 18, which converts to 9. A year, moreover, that by the nature of mathematics is a multiple of 9. Our late friend wasn't taking any chances getting married on an inauspicious day, which would have been any day not all wrapped up in 9s."

"Considering what happened five years later," the Inspector remarked, "our late friend's marital good-luck number had the whammy on it."

Ellery glanced at his father curiously. "Are you suggesting that his wife . . . ?"

"Who's suggesting?" the Inspector said. "Keep going, Ellery, you've got me fascinated. How else did he use those 9s of his?"

"The East Side apartment building Importuna

bought years ago. Its street number? 99. Number of floors? 9. Can there be any doubt that those 9s are why he bought the building? Or at least that he wouldn't have bought it unless the street number and the number of floors had been part and parcel of the property?

"The man was awesome in his consistency. One report comments that practically every article of Importuna's clothing bears his monogram, and that the monogram in every case — in *every* case — is not merely *NI* for Nino Importuna, but it has a strange little squiggle after the *I* in the design that looks like a small *n-e!* He wasn't satisfied with just the *NI*, you see; he had to have the 9 spelled out by an engraver's trick. This curious monogram — some of his correspondence refers to it as his crest — appears on his personal and business stationery, on his luggage, on his cars, on his planes, on his yachts — right up and down the line. Even his signature . . . have you seen his signature, dad, or facsimiles of it?"

"What about it?"

"Evidently you didn't notice. He always added a flourish to Importuna. A small flourish attached to the final *a* that, if you examine it carefully, looks remarkably like — you guessed it — a 9.

"To say that he was obsessive on the subject has to be a monumental understatement," Ellery exclaimed. "Do you know how he paced? How he paced! While dictating correspondence or memoranda, for instance, or thinking aloud — this is a tidbit I had from Peter Ennis — Importuna would take 9 steps one way, 9 steps back. Never more, never less. Ennis says he first noticed it because of a certain rhythm in Importuna's pacing, and he didn't realize the reason until one day he counted the steps."

"Oh, come on, now," Inspector Queen said. "That makes the guy a nut."

"Of course. Who but a magnificent nut could make that much money? Do you know that he wouldn't buy a set of books unless it consisted of 9 volumes, or 18, or 27, or some other multiple of 9? In his apartment you can find everything from *Extinct Birds of the New Hebrides* to *History of Gynecology*. Apparently to Importuna the important thing in his books was not their subject or contents, but their number."

"Look," his father said. "He was a nut about 9s. So all right. What I still want to know is, How are 9s going to help us poor flatfeet find his killer? How do the 9s enter into his 'murder'?"

"Ah," Ellery said, as if he had caught the old man by a debating point. "I don't know how they're going to help us find his killer, but that they enter into his murder is a *fact*. Is several facts, in fact."

"Say, that's right, isn't it?" the Inspector muttered. "I didn't put 2 and 2, I mean 4 and 5, or 6 and 3 — ah, forget it! — together. The time of the murder —"

"That's one of them, yes. The blow that struck

Importuna's wristwatch during the attack stopped the watch at 9 minutes past 9 o'clock. I wouldn't have believed it unless I'd seen the watch myself. And by the way, it's no accident that when Nino ordered that watch made for him he stipulated, as I'm sure he did, the use of rubies. Rubies, along with garnets and bloodstones, are considered lucky stones by people who are influenced by that sort of thing. Interestingly enough, you garner the luck when you wear the lucky gems next to your skin. Nothing can get closer to your skin than a wristwatch."

The Inspector was not so much silent as speechless. But finally he managed to say, "And the number of blows."

"Right, 9 distinct and separate skull fractures, from 9 blows. And Doc Prouty says he had to have been dead well before the 9th blow was delivered."

"But that's all the 9s in the murder."

"That's not all the 9s in the murder, dad. The weapon, that abstraction in cast iron. With that graceful loopy curve? Didn't you notice it has the general appearance of a number 9?

"So that's three 9-elements in the murder itself," Ellery declaimed to his feet as he blundered about pulling his nose, "and I refuse to accept even the mathematical possibility that they were coincidences. Death at 9:09 P.M., caused by a weapon in the shape of a 9, a weapon moreover that struck Importuna's head 9 times

. . ." Ellery shook his own head so vigorously it made his father's neck ache. "There's only one explanation that satisfies me: The killer, fully informed of Importuna's all-inclusive faith in the mystic qualities of 9, went out of his way to surround Importuna's murder — to infuse it, identify it, call attention to it — with 9s. I'm almost tempted to say, although I don't quite know why, to bury it under a pile of them. Note that he didn't have to hit his victim's head 9 times — Importuna was dead well before, according to the M.E.

"Was he satisfying his own passion for fantasy, for grotesquerie, some bizarre sense of the fitness of things, even things like murder? Nino having lived by the 9s, so to speak, the murderer thought he ought to die by the 9 as well?"

"I don't believe it," the Inspector snorted. "That would make Importuna's killer as cracked as Importuna. Two nuts in one case is one too much for me to swallow, Ellery."

"I'm with you."

"You are?" his father said, astounded.

"Certainly. Whatever else he is, the man who planned and executed that cock-eyed murder of Julio and then, after Marco hanged himself, pulled this 9 murder of Nino is a brain — a twisted brain, maybe, but a mighty sharp one. By killing Nino in the way he did, he threw those 9s in our faces. I can almost hear him laughing. Still, I get the queasy feeling that . . ."

"He's crazy!"

"You just said he can't be."

"So I've changed my mind," the old man exclaimed. "You know, a case like this could drive a whole police force nutty?"

Little did he know that the nuttiness had barely got off the ground.

And — in the stately language of the Inspector's youth — had he but known, he might have turned in his shield on the spot, dragging Ellery with him into the blessed crimelessness of some unsuspected isle of the poet's, in far-off seas.

The first of the anonymous messages (they could not be classified as anonymous letters since some were not written communications) arrived by first-class mail on the morning of Tuesday, September 19. It had been posted the previous day — the date on the envelope was September 18 — somewhere in the area served by the Grand Central postal station. The envelope was the ordinary medium-sized stamped type purchasable at any United States post office from Maine to Hawaii. It was addressed to Inspector Richard Queen, New York Police Department, Centre Street, New York, N.Y. 10013. The address had been inscribed, the experts said, by one of the hundreds of millions of blue-ink ball-point pens in daily use throughout the civilized world, and for that matter in some places not civilized. The writing was not script, which might have given them something to work on, but block-printed capital letters so meticulously featureless that they had no distinguishable character whatever and consequently provided nothing at all to work on.

The first comment Inspector Queen made when he saw the contents of the envelope was, "Why me?" The question was not altogether Joblike, in spite of the "O Lord" he was tempted to tack onto it. There were numerous other department brass involved in the Importuna investigation, some considerably more elevated in the hierarchy of command than Richard Queen. "Why me?" indeed? It seemed to portend fine deductions if only its inner meaning could be penetrated. But no one was to answer it until Ellery answered the other questions, too.

Curiously, there was not the smallest hesitation on the part of the Inspector in connecting the September 18th communication, cryptic as it appeared to the uninitiated, with the Impotuna murder. He linked them instantly, without benefit of Ellery, so well had he been briefed in the 9-ness of the case.

The Grand Central Station point of origin led nowhere (although later — after Ellery pointed out that its zip code was 10017, and that in all likelihood future messages from the anonymous sender would come through post offices whose zip codes also added up to 9 — there were hopes that stakeouts at such stations might result in a lucky grab. Succeeding messages from Anonymous did indeed come through the Triborough station, 10035, the Church Street station,

10008, and the Morningside station, 10026, but Anonymous remained ungrabbed).

No fingerprints or other identifiable marks were found on the contents of any of the envelopes. As for the envelopes themselves, what latents the print men developed could not be matched with the finger impressions of anyone directly or indirectly connected with Importuna, the Importunatos, or Importuna industries. They were eventually proved to have got on the envelopes through routine handling by specific postmen and postal clerks. An automatic check-out of the civil service employees involved turned up none with even a remote link to the Importuna family or organization.

When it was generally acknowledged that the first communication ("If you can call it that!" Inspector Queen groused to one of his superiors) was from the murderer they were massively seeking, the order came down from on high to keep its arrival and contents, indeed its very existence, confidential within the department, and even there only on a restricted need-to-know basis. Word was passed along from the office of the First Deputy Commissioner himself that any violation of this order resulting in a leak to the press or broadcast media would immediately be turned over to the Deputy Commissioner–Trials for severe disciplinary action. When other messages in the vein of the first were received, the injunction was repeated in even stronger terms.

What Inspector Queen pulled out of the commonplace envelope bearing the Grand Central Station postmark that morning of September 19 was part of a quite remarkable, crisp, never-played-with Bicycle-brand playing card with the red design on the back. What was remarkable about it was that the card had, with great care, been torn in half from side to side.

It was half a 9 of clubs.

The instant the Inspector spotted the figure 9 in the corner, a vision of 9 pips on a whole 9 of clubs flashed through his head. Thereupon he handled the half card as if it had been presoaked in a solution guaranteed to kill on contact.

"It's from Importuna's killer," the Inspector said to Ellery, who had winged to his father's office at the old man's call. "The 9-card tells us that."

"Not only the 9-card."

"There's something else?" his father said, nettled. He had expected a pat on the back for having learned his lesson so well.

"When was this mailed?"

"September 18, according to the postmark."

"The 9th month. And 18 adds up to 9. And I point out further," Ellery went on, "that Importuna was murdered on the 9th of September — 9 days before this was mailed."

The Inspector clasped his head. "I know I'm going to wake up any minute! . . . All right," he said, taking hold of himself. "A 9 of clubs torn in

163

half. The 9's as good as a trademark all by itself. I admit it, I admit the 9 days business, everything! This has to do with the Importuna case, no question about it. Only what, son, what?"

The silver eyes of the younger Queen held a glitter of high adventure. "Didn't you ever have your fortune told by cards in Coney Island?"

"Coney Island." His father chomped on the words as if he tasted them and they tasted foul. "Fortune-telling . . . No!"

"Fortune-telling yes. Each card of the 52 in the deck has its individual meaning, not duplicated by any of the others. For example, the 5 of diamonds in the modern referent system means a telegram. The jack of hearts indicates a preacher. The ace of spades —"

"I know that one, thanks," the Inspector said grimly. "What's the 9 of clubs supposed to mean?"

"Last warning."

"Last *warning?*" The Inspector chewed on it in a surprised way.

"But this doesn't mean last warning, dad."

"Make up your mind, son, will you? First you say it means last warning, then you say it doesn't mean last warning! Ellery, I'm in no mood for jokes!"

"I'm not joking. It means last warning when it's a whole 9 of clubs. But this one was torn in half. When a card is torn in half its meaning is reversed. That's the rule."

"The rule . . . reversed." The Inspector looked

dazed. "You mean . . . like . . . *first* warning?"

"That seems obvious."

"It does? Why? First warning about what?"

"I can't tell you."

"You can't? Why not?"

"I don't know."

"You don't *know?* Ellery, you can't march into my office and get off a lot of — of stuff about fortune-telling, and then leave me with my tonsils hanging out! I've got to make a report on this."

"I wish I could help you, dad. But I simply have no idea what he's warning you about. First *or* last."

The Inspector muttered, "Helpful Henry!" and hurried off with his mysterious clue to his fated rendezvous at Golgotha. It was only late that night, tossing from one side of his bed to the other, when he could no longer hide the memory of the day's subsequent developments, that it popped up in all its hideous clarity. Last warning . . . cut in half means first warning . . . What does that mean, Queen? . . . I don't know *what* it means, sir. . . . Doesn't that weirdo — I mean that son of yours have an opinion, Queen? This is his weirdo kind of case. . . . No, sir, Ellery doesn't. . . . Those growling executive voices and those concrete executive faces would constitute the stuff of many a future nightmare.

The second communication came in the same kind of envelope as the first, and it was similarly addressed to Inspector Queen. This one, however, yielded no playing card, half or whole. Instead, it contained a small sheet of cheap white paper, 4 inches by $5^7/_8$, which under magnification revealed fragments of glue and red-cloth binding on one of the short edges. The paper was unwatermarked.

"This sheet," the laboratory report said, "was torn off an ordinary memorandum pad of the type purchasable for 10¢ at any stationery, drug, or 5-and-10-cent store. It would be impossible to trace to its retail outlet, and even if it could be so traced . . ."

What was block-lettered in capitals by ball-point pen on the little sheet radiated no more light than the lab report:

ONE OF NINO'S BOYHOOD PALS
BECAME SUPREME COURT JUSTICE.

Unsigned.

The brass jury weighing the evidence of their eye brought in a verdict of nol-pros for Richard Queen; by this time briefed through the father by the son, they had come themselves to recognize the 9-man ship of the message even though its import conveyed absolutely nothing to any of them, including the briefer. So one of Nino's boyhood pals had made it all the way to the United States Supreme Court. Good for him, whoever he is, as the Deputy Commissioner in charge of Legal Matters commented sourly, but

I ask you, what of it? (No one considered for an instant that the Supreme Court referred to might be the Supreme Court of New York State, or of some other state, for that matter. After all, there was only one famous Supreme Court composed of 9 members.)

And the message itself contained 9 words.

"You know something?" the First Deputy Commissioner said. "Goddam it."

Nevertheless, sheer technique dictated that an inquiry be launched — officially, all police inquiries were launched — into "Nino's boyhood pals" and their ultimate destinations in life; and an investigation to that end was so ordered.

The third message was reminiscent of the first in that the envelope contained a new, red-backed Bicycle playing card.

But this time it was a whole card.

The 9 of hearts.

"I'll bite," Inspector Queen growled. "What does the 9 of hearts mean in fortune-telling?"

"Usually," Ellery replied, "disappointment."

"Disappointment? What's that supposed to mean? Whose disappointment?"

"He may be trying to tell us," Ellery said, pulling his nose so hard it brought tears to his eyes, "that it's going to be ours."

The next communication reverted to the more intelligible direct message:

EARLY CAREER NINO SEMIPRO
   SHORTSTOP
BINGHAMTON NEW YORK TEAM.

"Did Importuna ever play semipro ball?" the Inspector wanted to know.

"Are you asking me?" Ellery cried. "I don't know!" His responses tended to be uttered these days in very loud tones, as if he, or the world, or both, were going deaf.

"Just thinking out loud, son. Baseball teams take the field with —"

"With 9 men, yes. I've already *seen* that, thank you."

"And the message —"

"Composed of 9 words again. I've seen that, too. What I don't see is what all this *means*. Where it's *going*."

Memorandum to R. Queen, Inspector, from Lew B. Malawan, chief of detectives: *Institute investigation baseball career Nino Importuna or Tullio Importunato.*

"It's catching," the Inspector groaned. "9 words!"

The pattern persisted. The following message was again delivered in terms of a playing card, apparently from the same deck.

This time it was the 9 of spades.

"Grief," Ellery said.

"You're telling me?" the Inspector said. "But what I meant was, what's the 9 of spades mean?"

"I just told you. Grief."

"It *means* grief? That's all?"

"Well, obviously, grief for somebody."

"Who?"

"Whom," Ellery said. "I can't imagine. Or maybe I can. Virginia Importuna? After all, she did find herself divested of a husband in a particularly nasty way."

"But that doesn't get us anywhere, Ellery."

"I know. On the other hand, dad, I don't suppose the killer who's sending all these messages is especially eager for us to get anywhere. It's likelier he's trying to drive us into Loony Park."

"I think that's exactly what he's trying to do. For the ducks of it."

"I couldn't agree less."

"You just said he was!"

"Do you believe everything people say? These messages have a more rational purpose — a more *practical* one — than playing ring-a-lievio with the New York City Police Department. But the trouble is . . . for the life of me . . . Oh, hell, dad, I'm going back home and tackle my novel again."

"That thing still hanging around?" his father asked coldly.

Ellery slunk out.

NINO'S PALM SPRINGS RANCHO
HAS EXCELLENT PRIVATE
    GOLF COURSE.

Same type of envelope, same kind of paper, same capital lettering in similar ink by the same sort of pen.

No clues.

Nothing to follow up.

"Reads like a blasted real estate agent's ad," Ellery grumbled. "You see what he's driving at in this one, of course?"

"What am I, a dumdum? A 9-year-old — I mean a kid could figure it out," the Inspector said glumly. "Private golf courses usually have 9 holes."

"But even if Nino's has 18 —"

"I know, Ellery, 1 and 8 make 9."

"And exactly 9 words again in the message. God!" Ellery implored with no trace or tinge of impiety. "I wish . . . I *wish* I knew why this character is doing this!"

If the latest message smacked of real estate advertising, its successor ranged far, far afield — by accusation, at least, into the competence of Baron Richard von Krafft-Ebing:

NINO GOT HIS JOLLIES CAT OF
NINE TAILS WHIPPINGS.

"The question is," Ellery ruminated aloud, "does the late Mr. Importuna rest accused of being a devotee of Sacher-Masoch or of le Comte de Sade?"

"Wouldn't this make a juicy bit for the

newshounds," the Inspector said, shaking his head. "Do you suppose it's true?"

"How should I know?" Ellery asked crossly. "I wasn't privy to the secrets of Importuna's bedroom. Although why not? When you've got $500,000,000 to play around with, a conventional sex life might well seem too parochial. I wonder if this guy doesn't know any better, or cuts his cloth to measure."

"Sometimes you sound like a flea in a foreign dictionary," his father complained. "If who doesn't know any better?"

"The lad who's sending you all these informative messages. 'Nino got his jollies cat of nine tails whippings.' Note what he does. To get four of the 9 words he wants in this one, he separates the compound word *cat-o'-nine-tails* into its four components. I consequently ask, Doesn't he know any better, or was it a deliberate mistake of convenience? Not that it matters. But I'm desperate. Aren't you?"

"I'll buy that." Inspector Queen rose with the new message protected by a manila envelope. "Oh. Ellery, one thing. Why the devil is it called cat-o'-nine-tails?"

"Because the marks left on the victim's skin after a flogging, by the 9 cords that constitute the whip, are supposed to resemble scratches from a cat's claws. Of course, I don't testify to that as either a participant or an eyewitness. It's strictly hearsay."

"Then the hell with it." And Inspector Queen

left his office to report this latest development, stomping as he went.

"Wait! *Cat? 9 lives?*" Ellery cried to his father's dwindling back. "Don't forget to mention that one!"

Almost a week went by without an envelope.

"It's all over," the Inspector said hopefully. "He's through badgering me."

"No, daddy," Ellery said. "He's just letting out line. Don't you know when you're hooked?"

"But how can you be so sure there'll be more?" his father said, exasperated.

"There will be."

The next morning, there it was in the mail on the Inspector's desk:

NINO COMMISSIONED STATUES
OF MUSES FOR VILLA LUGANO ITALY.

"Bully for him," the Inspector muttered. "Muses? Can't be Mafiosi. I'd know the name."

"It goes back quite a way," Ellery said wearily. "The Muses, dad — the 9 Muses. The 9 daughters of Mnemosyne and Zeus. Calliope, Clio, Erato — it doesn't matter. Greek mythology."

The Inspector shaded his eyes with a quivering hand. "And, of course, again 9 words in the message. Did Importuna have a villa in Lugano?"

"What? Oh. Yes, I think so. No, I'm not sure. Ah, what difference does it make! This is a nightmare! And it's going to go on forever."

172

It was intended as a rhetorical statement, requiring no acknowledgment. Nevertheless, Ellery acknowledged it.

"No, it's not," he said. "There's going to be one more."

And two mornings later there was another envelope in the Inspector's mail, and he opened it in view of an audience. The audience consisted of Ellery and a very few of the more stable departmental brass who had been aroused by Ellery's prophecy.

Out fell a new red-backed Bicycle playing card.

A 9 of clubs.

"But he's already sent me a 9 of clubs," Inspector Queen protested, as if his anonymous correspondent had broken some rule of their mysterious game. "In his first envelope."

"He sent you half a 9 of clubs," Ellery said. "Quite different. By the way, this tells us one thing. To get a whole 9 of clubs after tearing a 9 of clubs in half, he had to go out and buy a second deck with the red backs."

"That makes a difference?" one of the lesser brass asked anxiously.

"Not the slightest," Ellery replied. "Simply noted it for the record. Well, gentlemen! You see what this means?"

There was a several-throated *"What?"*

"You recall, dad, I told you the meaning of a whole 9 of clubs."

The Inspector flushed in depth. "I, uh, forget."

"Last warning."

"That's right! Last warning. Of course. Last warning about what, Ellery? To whom?"

"Haven't the ghost of a glimmer."

The Inspector smiled feebly in the direction of his superiors, apologizing for the unsatisfactory performance of his progeny.

Roared the First Deputy Commissioner: "Doesn't *anybody* in this vooming place know *anything* about these bleepy, cronky, withertupping messages?"

Silence.

"If I may interject?" began Ellery.

"You don't even work here, Queen!"

"No, sir. But I'm in a position to assure you, Commissioner, this has been lover-boy's last message."

"How can you know that!"

"Because, sir," Ellery said, waving aloft all the fingers of his right hand and all but the thumb of his left, "this was the 9th one."

The days passed and there was no further messages, Ellery deriving a tiny satisfaction from the tiny triumph. These days he was finding himself grateful for crumbs. For example, he was the first of those privileged to be in on the secret of the messages' very existence to point out that, with the initial envelope having been posted on Monday, September 18, and the 9th envelope on Sunday, October 15, the period spanned by the 9 messages was precisely 27 days.

And 27 was a multiple of 9.

And 2 plus 7 equaled 9.

While through his head ran the leitmotif of his existence these days: *He's deluging us with 9s. Why?*

Inspector Queen read, and reread, and rereread reports old and new until he could have repeated them perfectly with his eyes shut in a photographer's darkroom. None of them revealed the faintest streak of light in the absolute night of the case.

An early theory that Nino Importuna might have been murdered by poison before being struck on the head was not borne out by the toxicological examination of his internal organs. The cause of his gastric distress a few hours before his death was traced to a culinary crisis that, at worst, might have cost the late multimillionaire the services of his temperamental chef.

For a preliminary course of the birthday-and-anniversary dinner, Mrs. Importuna days before had ordered César to prepare one of her husband's favorite dishes, *cacciucco alla Livornese*, a Leghorn seafood stew two of whose ingredients were lobster and squid. For this Italian recipe César always insisted on going to the source, and the lobster and squid were flown in from Italy. César prepared the sauce first, in which he then simmered the squid and lobster. When he tasted the result, he howled in anguish. The squid, he bellowed, had a *guasto gusto,* a bad taste; he would positively not proceed with the *cacciucco;* indeed, his honor as a chef was at stake, and he threatened to quit in humiliation. Importuna himself had come into the kitchens in the emergency; he had swallowed a substantial sampling of the squid; he had cast his vote unhesitatingly with César who, mollified, withdrew his resignation. The *cacciucco* was ousted from the dinner menu. César had experienced a very slight stomach distress later that evening, at roughly the same time as Importuna had the severer attack. Unfortunately, the contents of the casserole had been ground up in the waste-disposer, so no analysis of it could be made. However, a trace of the cephalopod flesh had been found in Importuna's stomach, and laboratory examination indicated that he had suffered a nonlethal, indeed rather mild, food poisoning. The spoiled squid could have nothing to do with his subsequent murder.

Another theory, advanced by those on the inside who believed the anonymous messages to be the work of a crank unconnected with the case and thus irrelevant, was that Nino Importuna and his brother Julio — perhaps all three brothers — had been entangled with the Mafia. (The Mafia theorists made much of the *siciliano* origin of the Importunato clan, building their argument on a sort of guilt-by-geography.) According to these officers, the Mafia had wormed its way into some of Importuna Industries' operations, and the murders of the brothers had resulted from the inevitable power struggle over control of the great conglomerate.

The theory did not survive investigation. No evidence of any sort was adduced to connect Nino, Marco, or Julio, or any of their companies, with Cosa Nostra. This was the consensus not only of the Central Investigation Bureau and other New York City experts in the field of organized crime, but it was the burden as well of the information passed along to Centre Street by the FBI.

If the lack of progress in the Importuna-Importunato case was frustrating to Inspector Queen and his fellow officers, Ellery acted as if it were a personal affront. His novel, long since all but given up for lost by his publisher, continued to molder on his desk. He was sleeping badly, jerking awake at the climaxes of horrid dreams in which 9s loomed large, but the details of which he could not retain in his conscious memory for more than a second or two no matter how desperately he tried; he picked at his food like a man suffering from iron-poor blood and found himself losing weight his lean figure could not spare; and he snapped at everybody, including his father and poor Mrs. Fabrikant, who crept about the Queen apartment these days looking chronically as if she were about to burst into tears.

"It's a pleasure to see a living face, even if it's a chin-dragger," Doc Prouty said. "We get to see

177

mostly dead ones around here. How you been, Ellery? What can I do you for?" The Medical Examiner was of Inspector Queen's generation and, like the Inspector, he was a walking museum of its fossil humor.

"Chin-dragging, as you diagnosed. As for what you can do, tell me about the time of Nino Importuna's death." Ellery looked away from the M.E., who was chewing on a peanut-butter-and-tuna sandwich from a rusty lunchbox on his desk. For as long as Ellery could recall, Sam Prouty had brought his lunch to work. Ellery had nothing against bringing honest lunches to work, but he had always felt that Doc Prouty's working environment was not exactly suited to the practice.

"Time of Nino Importuna's death." The M.E. squinted as he masticated. "What is this, Archaeology Week? That's ancient history."

"I know, the blow to Importuna's wrist stopped his watch at 9:09. What I mean is, did 9:09 P.M. prove consistent with your autopsy finding?"

"Have you any idea how many posts we've performed around here since we did him?"

"Don't give me that, doc. You can remember the details of posts you did 20 years ago."

"It's all in my report, Ellery. Didn't you read it?"

"It was never shown to me. How about answering my question?"

"That 9:09 on the watch was a lot of bunk. It's

our medical opinion Importuna was beaten to death around midnight of that night — in fact, a bit later than midnight. Just about three hours later than the watch showed."

Life stirred in the silvery depths of Ellery's eyes. "Do you mean his wristwatch was preset and deliberately stopped at 9:09 to confuse the issue as to the time of his death?"

"Mine not to reason why. That's somebody else's department. Anyway, why I give out my official findings to a squirt civilian on demand this way, like some damned information clerk, I'll never figure out. Want a piece of this sand-wich? The old lady makes a mean peanut-butter-and-tuna."

"I'd rather starve than deprive you of a morsel of it. Oh! I may assume — or may I? — that you found nothing in the course of your postmortem to change your original count of 9 blows to Importuna's head?"

"I said 9, and it was 9."

"Well, thanks, Doc. I'll leave you to enjoy the corpses of all those little peanuts." Ellery turned back. "One other thing. The clout that stopped Importuna's watch: Am I correct in believing that it was an extension of one of those 9 blows to his head? That is, that one of the blows to his head glanced off and struck his wrist — maybe because he threw his arm up in a reflexive attempt to ward off the blow?"

"Did I say that?" Dr. Prouty demanded through a spray of peanut butter and tuna fish.

"I'm saying it. I mean, I'm not *saying* it, I'm merely asking if that isn't what happened."

"Well, it isn't. Not in my opinion. The crack on the wrist that broke his watch came from a different blow altogether. There wasn't a trace of blood or head hair or brain tissue on the watch or his wrist. In fact — if you want to know what I really think — I think the blow that broke the watch was even delivered by a different weapon. *Not* that iron sculpture whatsit."

"Was this in your report, Doc?"

"Certainly not! I'm a pathologist, not a detective. My report said there was no blood, hair, or tissue on the watch or wrist, period. That was a proper medical observation. Anything beyond that is somebody else's job."

"I'm losing my miggies," Ellery muttered, smiting his brow. "Why didn't I insist on reading your autopsy report?"

And he departed on the run, leaving the medical examiner with his dentures sunk to their foundations in the dead body of an apple.

Virginia Whyte Importuna received him in the sitting room of her private quarters in the penthouse. He was surprised to find the room done in early Colonial American, like hundreds of thousands of American homes; he had rather expected the Grand Style of *Le Roi Soleil*, or 18th century Venetian lacquer and gessowork.

But what he had at first thought were good reproductions he soon recognized as originals in priceless condition. There was a 17th century press cupboard of oak, pine, and maple, for example, which he could have sworn was stolen from the Metropolitan Museum of Art, and even earlier Brewster-type chairs that looked as if they might have belonged to Governor William Bradford. Every piece in the young widow's sitting room was an antique of great rarity.

"I see you're admiring my antiques, Mr. Queen," Virginia said.

"Admiring is scarcely the word, Mrs. Importuna. I'm overcome."

"I had these rooms done over — my private apartment — the first year I was married. My husband gave me free rein. I'm New England on my father's side going way, way back, and I've always doted on the furniture and artifacts and things of pre-Revolutionary America. But it was the first time in my life I had the means to collect them."

"Your husband was very generous with you, I take it."

"Oh, yes," she said quickly. Too quickly? He was interested by the way she immediately changed the subject, as if she were reluctant to discuss Nino Importuna. "I'm sorry you had such a hard time getting up to see me, Mr. Queen. Sometimes I feel like the princess in the fairy tale who's kept locked in the tower and guarded by dragons. I own I don't know how many homes all over the world, they tell me, most of which I've never visited, and they won't even let me stick my little toe out of this building. I'm beginning to hate 99 East. How long does this have to go on?"

"Until there's a significant break in the case, I imagine," Ellery said. "Well. I don't want to take up too much of your time —"

"Heavens, I have more of it than I know what to do with." Virginia sighed and looked down at the hands in her lap. The instant she did, they stopped wriggling. "Aside from having to sign thousands of papers the lawyers push in front of me, I don't get to do very much of anything these days. It's a pleasure to be able to talk to somebody who isn't a policeman."

"Then I'm afraid I'm going to be a disappointment to you," Ellery said, smiling. Why was she so nervous? Surely by this time she must be hardened to such encounters. "Even though I'm not a policeman, Mrs. Importuna, I'm here to ask you some policemanlike questions."

"Oh."

He thought it disingenuous of her, the little note of surprise and regret. She must know that he had not sought her out to discuss antiques.

"Do you mind?"

She shrugged. "I should be used to it, but I'm not. Of course I mind, Mr. Queen. I mind very much. However, it's not going to do me much good, is it?"

And that was clever of her.

Ellery felt the familiar flow of adrenalin at the prospect of a battle of wits.

"Since we're being so candid with each other, Mrs. Importuna — no, it's not. You can always refuse to answer, naturally. But I don't see why you should, unless you have something to hide."

"What is it you want to know?" she asked abruptly.

"That cast-iron sculpture the murderer used to kill your husband. Was it usually kept in Mr. Importuna's bedroom?"

"It was never kept in his bedroom. He didn't like it."

"Oh? Where was it kept, then?"

"In the master living room."

"I don't understand, Mrs. Importuna. That could be an important piece of information. I've read the transcripts of most if not all of your interrogations, and I don't recall your revealing that fact before. Why didn't you?"

"Nobody ever asked me the question before, that's why!" The ethereal blue of her eyes showed flashes now, like water struck by the sun; there was warm color on her cheekbones, giving her the look of a doll. "I assumed . . . Well, I suppose I just didn't think about it."

"Unfortunate. Because you see where this leads us, Mrs. Importuna. Whoever it was, while on his way to your husband's bedroom to commit the murder, paused in the living room long enough to select the weapon with which to commit it. Apparently he didn't bring one with him, a gun or a knife; or, if he did come armed, he deliberately chose the sculpture in the living room instead. Which raises the interesting corollary question. Why that sculpture? I've seen a dozen objects in the master living room — and in Mr. Importuna's bedroom, for that matter — that could have served the killer's purpose just as well. Come to think of it, he didn't have to go through the master living room to get to your husband's room. Meaning that he went out of his way to get his hands on that sculpture. Why would he do that? What was so important about the cast-iron abstract?"

"I wouldn't know."

"Not even a theory, Mrs. Importuna?"

"No."

"Did the shape of that sculpture ever strike you particularly? Remind you of anything?"

She shook her head.

"Well, it doesn't matter," Ellery said, smiling again. "Tell me about it, Mrs. Importuna."

"I don't know what there is to tell . . ."

"I believe you said that it wasn't kept in Mr. Importuna's bedroom because he didn't like it —"

"That's not what I said at all. I made two separate statements, Mr. Queen. One: It wasn't kept in my husband's room. Two: He didn't like it. There's no because in between."

"Oh, I see. Where did it come from?"

"It was a gift."

"To Mr. Importuna?"

"No."

"To you?"

"Yes."

"And it usually stood in the living room, you said."

"Yes, fitted into an ebony stand."

"May I ask what the occasion for the gift was? And who gave it to you?"

"It was a birthday gift. Two years ago. As for who gave it to me, Mr. Queen, I don't see that that has the least bearing on anything we're discussing."

"It's been my experience," Ellery said chattily, "that you never quite know in advance what's going to turn out to be important and what isn't. Although I grant the odds are usually that any given fact is of no importance whatever. But I sense resistance, Mrs. Importuna. This arouses my curiosity — I've got a lot of cat in me. If you won't tell me who presented you with the sculpture, I assure you I, can find out. And I intend to do so. As the saying goes, I have my methods."

"Peter Ennis." It was a flat statement, wrung out of her, juiceless.

"Thank you," Ellery murmured. "I can see why you preferred not to reveal the source of the gift. Ennis has been virtually living here in his capacity of confidential secretary to your husband and your husband's brothers. He's a personable, virile, attractive young man, tall, Nordic, the perfect male counterpart, in fact, of the young and very beautiful lady of the house. Who was married to a squat, ugly old man. If it became known that the young secretary was giving the young wife valuable gifts, people

185

might talk. Servants certainly would. And Mr. Importuna? Did the husband know that the valuable sculpture was a gift to his wife from his secretary?"

"No, he didn't! I lied to him! I told him I bought it for myself!" Her shining hair seemed suddenly in disarray; she looked oddly undressed. "You're a cruel man, Mr. Queen, do you know that? Nino was jealous. I didn't have the easiest marriage in the world. There are circumstances about my marriage that —"

She stopped.

"Yes?" Ellery prodded her gently.

But she was shaking her locks, smiling. "You're also smart as all get-out, Mr. Queen. I don't believe I'm going to continue this conversation." She rose and walked over to the door. "Crump will see you out."

She pulled on the bell rope.

"I'm sorry I've upset you, Mrs. Importuna. If you knew me better, you'd know I'm really not cruel, just death on rats. Would you mind telling me one thing more?"

"It depends on what it is."

"Sculptures, like paintings, are usually titled. Does the sculpture Peter Ennis gave you have a name?"

"Yes. What was it again? Something icky. . . . It's inscribed on the base of the stand — a little plaque . . ." She frowned; but then the frown lifted like fog and her face turned sunny. At that moment she was extraordinarily innocent in her loveliness. "I remember! *Newborn Child Emerging.*"

Ennis, you dog, Ellery thought.

Crump did not see Ellery out. His stately British march said that he had every intention of doing so, but Ellery stopped him after ten paces. "I want to talk to Mr. Ennis before I leave. Is he in?"

"I can see, sir." Unexpectedly, Crump's tone suggested that he thought it a jolly idea.

"Please do."

Crump knew all about them, then, and of course he disapproved. There was no more straitlaced lot than the old-fashioned servitor class, in the front rank of whom stood the butlers.

"Mr. Ennis states that he is too busy, sir."

"By a coincidence, I'm busy, too. We'll be busy together. Which way, Crump?"

"Mr. Ennis states, sir . . ." Crump's tone this time suggested occupational regret, a what-can-I-do-sir-I-can-only-follow-orders apologia.

"I'll take you off the hook, Crump. Where is he?"

"Thank you, sir. This way, Mr. Queen."

He led Ellery briskly, with visible enjoyment, to Nino Importuna's den. There, enthroned in his late employer's chair behind the Medici table, sat the handsome confidential secretary; he was up to his elbows in files and documents. Peter Ennis looked away from his paper work and expressed annoyance without hesitation.

"I told Crump to tell you I was too busy to see you, Queen. I simply haven't the time to go over the same dreary old ground with you. Crump, I'll have to report you to Mrs. Importuna for this."

"Then you'll be persecuting an innocent man," Ellery said in his best *amicus curiae* manner. "Crump performed his duty with the fidelity of any Englishman. I had to use muscle to get him to bring me here. Verbal muscle, of course. I don't believe you'll be needed further, Crump; thank you. May I sit down, Ennis? This will take some time. No? I get the feeling you'd rather not talk to me."

"All right," Peter said, shrugging. "I don't have to put up with you, Queen; I'm doing this only to get rid of you. You've no official status — I can't imagine how you weaseled your way up here, the way that lobby's patrolled."

"It's all in the wrist action." Ellery seated himself in the squat, lumpily carved visitor's chair and immediately wished he hadn't. "Whoever selected this chair had a bit of the old Inquisition spirit in him. Importuna, I suppose. Speaking of whom: Did he have an old friend, someone going all the way back to his boyhood, who grew up to become a justice of the United States Supreme Court?"

"If he did, he never mentioned it to me."

"Then let me put it this way: To your knowledge, did Importuna ever communicate — by letter, phone, Pony Express, however — with any justice of the Supreme Court?"

"To my knowledge? No."

"Did any justice of the Supreme Court ever communicate with him?"

Peter grinned. "You're cool, man, you know that? You don't let go. No, not to my knowledge. What's this about a Supreme Court justice?"

"Did he play semipro baseball as a young man? Under the name of Nino Importuna, Tullio Importunato, or some other name?"

"Baseball? Nino Importuna?" Peter's grin widened. "If you'd known him, Queen, you'd realize what a ridiculous question that is."

"Ridiculous or not, you haven't answered it."

"He failed to mention any such terrible secret of his past, at least to me. And I've never run across anything in his personal files to indicate it." The grin faded as Peter stared across the table. "I believe you're serious."

"Does Binghamton, New York, strike a bell?"

"In connection with Mr. Importuna? Binghamton? Not a tinkle."

Ellery mumbled to himself. Finally he said, "Now tell me he doesn't — didn't — own a rancho in Palm Springs, California."

"That he does — did."

"Really? You mean I've struck something at last?" Ellery hitched forward. "A property with a private golf course attached?"

"Golf course? Who on earth told you that?"

"Is there a golf course on the Palm Springs property!"

189

"Jumping down my throat will get you nowhere, Queen. You can't blame me for being surprised by such a question. You people haven't done your homework on Nino Importuna, have you? He'd no more consider setting foot on a golf course than becoming den mother of the neighborhood Girl Scouts. Considered golf a criminal waste of a grown man's time, especially a businessman. No, Nino didn't own a golf course in Palm Springs, or anywhere else. He didn't own a set of clubs. In fact, I don't believe he even knew how to play."

Ellery was pinching the tip of his nose to inflict "the pain that kills pain." "Did you ever happen to see a cat-o'-nine-tails in Importuna's effects?"

"See a *what?*"

We've received a tip that Nino Importuna was rather fond of whips and whippings. How say you, Mr. Confidential Secretary?"

Peter threw his head back. "I wasn't that confidential, I assure you!" Then he stopped laughing. "If you've got to pry into his sexual hang-ups, you've come to the wrong boy. The obvious source would be his wife, but I hope — in fact, I'm pretty sure — she'll spit in your eye."

"I had a conversation with Mrs. Importuna just now, and from something she let drop I gathered that their marital-sex relationship wasn't exactly —"

"I'm not going to discuss what isn't my business," Peter said loftily, "or yours. Please."

"Was Importuna a chaser? You should certainly know something about that."

"Chaser? Why, he was imp—" He stopped, stricken.

"Impotent?" Ellery said softly.

"I shouldn't have blurted that out? It could only have concerned Mrs. Importuna. Won't you forget I said it? But, of course, you won't."

"But of course. How do you know Importuna was impotent? Did he tell you? No, a man doesn't reveal a thing like that about himself to a younger, virile man, especially a little Napoleon like Nino Importuna. So you probably found out about it from his wife. Right?"

"I'm not saying another word on the subject!"

Ellery waved the subject away with instant amiability. "Here's one that shouldn't strain your milk: Did Importuna commission some sculptor to do the 9 Muses for his villa in Lugano? By the way, he did own a villa in Lugano, didn't he?"

"Yes, but I don't know anything about his commissioning sculptures for the place. And that's just the kind of thing I'd know all about, because it would have been my job to take charge of such a project and follow through on it. No runs, no hits, and lots of errors, Queen. Or do you want to go another inning or two?"

"I'm beginning to think someone's monkeying with the rules," Ellery grumbled. "Another question or so, Ennis and I'll leave you in peace, which is more than I can promise myself. Did

Importuna like cards? You know — poker, chemin de fer, bridge, faro, pinochle, canasta, gin — any card game at all?"

"He had absolutely no interest in cards or any other form of gambling. Except the stock market, and the way he played that it was more an art than a game of chance."

"How about cards to tell fortunes by?"

"Fortune-telling? Somebody's been feeding you boys LSD. Nino Importuna didn't tell fortunes, he was too busy making them."

"Who's Mr. E?"

"You do hop around." Peter stirred. "Mr. E? Now that the Importuna empire's in the throes of liquidation, I don't see any harm in telling you. For as long as I've been employed here, Mr. E has acted as Importuna's personal, confidential business investigator — his secret agent, you might call him. Whenever the boss became interested in a new business enterprise — whether he sensed that it was on the rise, or on the skids, and in either event might be bought cheap — any business venture that looked promising, he'd send Mr. E to look into it. No matter where it happened to be. Mr. E practically lives on planes, though he does his share of camel-riding, too. He's always reported to Mr. Importuna in person — and in private. To no one else, not even Julio or Marco."

"What's his name? It can hardly be just E."

"No, the E's an initial, I gather, but I haven't the foggiest idea to what. Mr. Importuna never told me, the name doesn't occur in his personal memoranda, and my work hasn't involved me with the man beyond making appointments for him to see the big boss."

"When Importuna wanted to get in touch with Mr. E, how did he address him? He had to address him by some name."

"No, he didn't. He used a code word, like a cable address. Had such code addresses in major cities all over the world. I've given all this information to the police, by the way. I thought they confide in you."

"Not necessarily on this one." Ellery sighed. "This Mr. E sounds mysterious."

"Big business has always been a mystery to me," Peter Ennis said. "By the way, Queen, speaking of mysteries, as long as I've allowed you to waste this much of my time . . . would you solve a mystery for me? It's been bothering the life out of me ever since it happened, and you have a reputation for this sort of thing."

"You won't prove it by my performance in this case," Ellery said. "What sort of thing?"

"It happened this past summer — back in June, I think it was. Mr. Importuna was dictating to me in here, and while he was pacing he suddenly stopped, glared at that bookshelf there, and then whirled and tore into me as if he'd caught me with my hand in his wallet. Seems I'd noticed several books standing upside down, and being a compulsively neat guy, like the fellow in *The Odd Couple*, I turned them right side up. Well, he really let me have it. Turned the books back upside down and reminded me that he'd warned me never to touch anything on that particular shelf — even put the blame for a deal's falling through on the fact that I disobeyed his order. It's bugged me ever since. What the devil's so special about those books that he considered them bad luck standing right side up, as in any self-respecting library?"

Ellery pounced on the reversed volumes.

"*The Founding of Byzantium* . . . MacLister . . ." He read the title page and scanned the first few pages of the text; he made similar examinations of Beauregard's *The Original KKK* and the Santini book, *The Defeat of Pompey*.

Replacing them as he had found them, Ellery riffled through some of the volumes that were stacked normally on the shelf.

He turned back to Peter, shaking his head. "Importuna was the obsessionist supreme. What a stamp collector he'd have made! Was he particularly interested in history?"

"Hell, no. As a matter of fact, he hardly read anything but market and business reports. I don't know why he bought any of these books, except that a study's supposed to have books."

"There's more to these three volumes than shelf fillers, Ennis. No mystery about it, if you start from how hipped he was on the subject of 9s. The MacLister book purports to prove by archaeological evidence that the city of Byzantium was founded in 666 B.C."

"666 B.C.?" For a moment Peter Ennis looked blank. Then light dawned. "Upside down, 666 becomes 999!"

Ellery nodded. "You reverted it to 666 by turning it right side up. That's about as idolatrous a crime as you can commit against a 9-worshiper, tampering with his mystique.

"The Santini book similarly. It's about the defeat of Pompey by the Parthian emperor Mithridates in 66 B.C. The 66 should have read 99 in Importuna's view; that's the way he set it, but with the temerity of ignorance you turned it back around to the invidious — even worse, meaningless — 66. No wonder he blew his top.

"The case of *The Original KKK* is of especially enchanting interest. The original Ku Klux Klan was formed the year after the Civil War ended, 1866. If you turn the volume upside down, every mention of 1866 comes out 9981. Add the integers making up 9981 — 9, 9, 8, and 1 — and you get 27; and 2 plus 7 comes down to that old black magic 9. Upside down the number 1866 represented to Nino the almost perfect number, like the date of his birth. By putting *The Original KKK* back right side up, you changed every one of its beautiful 9981s into 1866s, which add up to a mere 21, or 2 plus 1, or 3. Now 3 has been the magic number for a great many folks for thousands of years, but it didn't happen to be the number that turned your boss on. Only 9 could do that. I'm surprised he didn't fire you on the spot."

195

Peter waved faintly. "I'm dreaming this. The man was mad."

"Somebody said — who was it? — the *Tristram Shandy* man, Sterne, that's it — that madness is consistent, which is more than can be said of reason; or words to that effect. Do you want to see," Ellery demanded, "how the consistency of Importuna's kind of madness operated? Here's a book on the same shelf, *The Landing of the Pilgrims*. Standing right side up. Any particular reason for that? Oh, yes! The landing at Plymouth Rock took place Anno Domini 1620. The number 1620 is made up of 1 and 6 and 2 and 0, which total that indispensable 9. The number 1620 is also evenly divisible by 9, to the tune of 180 times. But 180 is 1 plus 8 plus 0, which gives you 9 again! Can't you see Importuna rubbing his hands in glee?"

"Truthfully," Peter muttered, "no. You really couldn't call him the gleeful type."

"You're nit-picking. Well, look at this one, Peter — may I call you Peter? I feel as if I've known you for a long time. *Magna Carta at Runnymede*, it's called. Hardly necessary to look inside. King John reluctantly signed the Great Charter, as every schoolboy knows, in the year 1215. Add, and what do you get? 1, 2, 1, and 5 give you 9. And is 1215 divisible by 9? You bet your sweet bippy — it produces the quotient 135. And 135? Why, 1 and 3 and 5 — again — make 9. Another 9-victory for the great tycoon.

"Or this fellow, Peter, also at attention in the

orthodox position. *The Establishment of the Roman Empire.* Done to his historic glory by Augustus Caesar after his victory at Actium four years earlier. Date of his establishment of the principate? 27 B.C. Good old 27. Doesn't produce quite the best results, but they're not bad. 2 and 7, of course, make 9. And 27 is evenly divided by 9. True, it doesn't give you a quotient of 9, but then you can't have everything, can you?

"The fact is, Peter," Ellery said, "every last book on this shelf, either in its upside down or its right side up position, is relevant to Importuna's mystical belief in the happy powers of 9. That's why he warned you not to touch any of them. That's why he got so angry when you did."

"I knew he considered 9 his good-luck number," Peter said, "but this . . . ! It's mumbo jumbo!"

"Oh, I don't know. You said something before about his accusing you of having caused a deal to fall through. Tell me, Peter, what if anything happened after Importuna restored that trinity of history books to the 9-favoring position? Because I'm sure, Importuna having been the man he was, he didn't let the failure of the deal go at that, once he knew why it had failed."

"You're right enough about that. He immediately set up a transatlantic conference call and arranged to make the other parties a new offer."

"What happened?"

"He raised the deal from the dead."

"You see?" Ellery said; and he shook Peter's hand in triumph and left.

At Police Headquarters Ellery learned that the lines out of Centre Street were still without a twitch. In spite of a second anonymous message to have achieved the high confidential fishing expedition into the awesome precincts of the Supreme Court, the Washington phase of the inquiry elicited no flicker or gleam of "the one of Nino's boyhood pals," living or dead, who was alleged by the second anonymous message to have achieved the high court bench. And the intelligence in the fourth message that the late multimillionaire had played in his youth for the Binghamton, New York, semiprofessional base-ball team raised echoes neither in Binghamton nor anywhere else.

There was no golf course on or abutting the Importuna property in Palm Springs, California. There had never been a golf course on or near the property. The claim of the sixth communication was simply false.

As far as could be determined, the allegation of the seventh letter was also false; at least it was unproved. Nino Importuna may or may not have been addicted to sadistic or masochistic sexual practices, but no evidence of any sort turned up corroborating the charge that he enjoyed the use of a cat-o'-nine-tails; and Mrs. Importuna, who was presumed to have been in the logical position to know, and who refused to discuss any aspect of her conjugal relationship with her late husband, nevertheless on the point specifying the cat-o'-nine-tails stated with some heat that "as far as I'm concerned, and to the best of my knowledge, it's an evil lie."

Further, the Importuna villa in Lugano displayed no images of the Muses, nor could any sculptor be located who would admit to having been commissioned to create such images, as stated by the eighth anonymous message.

"I guess the guy has to be a crank at that," Inspector Queen said. "We've had a meeting on it, and it's been just about decided to drop that whole line of inquiry."

"I don't think that would be wise," Ellery said, "but don't ask me why. Oh, two things, dad. I'd like a rundown on the building at 99 East — details of the sale to Importuna, a copy of the deed, and so on."

"What could that have to do with anything?"

"Call it hunch time. The other thing — no, I can take care of that myself."

"Of what?"

"I'll cable that private investigating agency I've been using in Italy to have a copy made of Tullio Importunato's baptismal certificate, from the church records, and airmail it to me."

"What for? Never mind," the Inspector grumped, "call it hunch time twice. What did you find out at the penthouse?"

Ellery looked at his father. "How did you

know I found out anything at the penthouse?"

"I haven't had to look at your pan all these years without being able to read it occasionally."

"I didn't find out anything, really. But it's more than a hunch. It's my considered opinion, what with this and that, that Virginia Importuna and Peter Ennis were planting a healthy set of horns on old Nino's head. I'm ready to take my oath it's consisted of more than a yearning glance now and then across the width of a room. Now tell me what's revived you."

"Revived? Me?"

"A few days ago you were ready to retire to an old folks' home. Today you have a viable look. What's been going on around here?"

"Well, we're working on something," the Inspector said cautiously. "It's actually been in the cards from the start. . . . It's all very hush-hush, Ellery, by direct order from the top; they could have my shield if they found out I've told even you."

"Told me what? You haven't told me a thing!"

"Well, it's still pretty tentative, son — we're inching our way along. I'll tell you this: We won't jump until we get the go-ahead from the D.A. Who's going to be almighty interested, by the way, in what you just told me. It could fit like a tight shoe."

"But what is it?"

To which the Inspector shook his head; and all Ellery's blandishments could not persuade the old sleuth to expatiate.

This was the autumn of his discontent.

Ellery doodled 9s; he dreamed them; he ate them like alphabet soup. He kept going over the 9 anonymous messages, searching like a monkey mother after lice for secret meanings . . . wondering if he should not consult a high-ranking cryptographer.

At this he balked, and not only because of the secrecy imposed by Centre Street. Even to consider such a far-out folly, he decided, was a measure of his frustration.

At times he felt, across the millennia of fictitious time, an empathy with the legendary son of Aegeus and Aethra as he groped through the labyrinth under the historic palace of Minos in Knossos toward a monster only dimly imagined. The trouble is, Ellery thought, I'm no Theseus, and I have no loving Ariadne to help me find the Minotaur. The number 9, unlike Ariadne's clew, was circuitous; started at any point, it led round and round, arriving nowhere.

He was positive of only one thing: The 9s meant something. It was inconceivable to him that they could have no meaning at all. The choice of the 9-symbolism by the prime mover of the murderous events was a pregnant fact.

Pregnant? Pregnancy?

For some reason the concept remained with him. He could not quite place the finger of his mind on the reason; but there it dangled, just tantalizingly out of reach.

If the whole case was like a pregnancy, was there going to be a stillbirth? Or was the lady in the painful process of aborting? Or was she going to go to term and throw her get in some sorry delivery room, producing one of those rare little monsters the doctors tacitly allow to die?

A 9-month monster.

9 . . .

Or 99? . . . 999? . . . 9,999? . . . 99,999? . . .

Along that route lay madness.

Meanwhile, back at 240 Centre Street, progress was being made, but inchmeal. Certain lines of investigation had now been closed off; that was considered progress, too, although not by the Police Commissioner and other exalted taskmasters. The anonymous messages had been officially written off, to Ellery's dismay. Exhaustive inquiries into Nino Importuna's business enemies, an impressive list, had consistently led to exhausted inquirers and nothing more. True, there was no trace as yet of the enigmatical Mr. E, who seemed to have been engulfed in some convulsion of nature. That line was being held open, but only as a matter of routine caution.

One day late in October Inspector Queen announced to Ellery, "Son, the time's come."

"For what?" Ellery mumbled. He mumbled a great deal these days.

"Remember all that highfalutin', complicated garbage you spilled after Julio Importunato's murder? About the shifting of the desk, and the left-handedness business, and how Marco was

202

being framed, and the Lord knows what else? It was great, Ellery. Only it was phony baloney. When Marco confessed to Julio's murder by committing suicide, down the drain went your fancy deductions."

"Thanks, dad," the son said. "A visit to your office these days really sets a fellow up."

"And stop sucking your thumb. Well, this time there's no call for mental flip flops. We've all let ourselves be euchred away from what's been under our noses, plain as daylight at 20,000 feet, from the beginning."

"I must be going blind. What's been under our noses?"

"For one thing, the motive."

"The motive?"

"For Importuna's murder," the Inspector said impatiently. "Aren't you with it today, Ellery? You once threw cooey-something at me —"

"Cui bono."

"That's it. Who benefits. Right? Well, that's so simple it hurts: The one who benefits, the *only* one who benefits, is Virginia Whyte Importuna. To the tune of half a *billion* smackers, for God's sake. That's a powerful lot of smackers. I guess when there's that much moola on the line," the Inspector philosophized, "it kind of dazzles you. Puts spots before your eyes. Anyway, as a rider to what I just said, not only did her husband's murder put half a billion smackers in Mrs. Importuna's pocket, but it's a fact that he was knocked off *just after she became his sole heir.* The ink on his new will was hardly dry. Right?"

"Right," Ellery said, "but —"

"No buts. That takes care of motive. How about opportunity, like you always put it?"

"As I always put it," Ellery said mechanically.

"Like, as, what's the difference? All right, how about opportunity? Nothing to it. Virginia could have marched into hubby's room bigger than life any time she wanted that night. Who could have got in there easier or more naturally? Who had a better right? Okay?"

"Okay," Ellery said, "but that's no argument at all. I still want to make the point —"

"Third, the weapon. And what is it? A hunk of cast-iron sculpture that belongs to her."

"Which the killer went out of his way — I beg your pardon, her way — to lay hands on for the purpose subsequently displayed, the killing of Importuna. Why didn't she leave a signed confession pinned to his pajamas? That would have been even more brilliant."

"Maybe the gender of your pronoun is still right," Inspector Queen said, his forefinger alongside his nose.

"What's that mean?"

"The secretary."

"Peter Ennis? That's always possible, of course, especially if the D.A. can produce proof that they've been having an affair. On the other hand, there's well-established testimony that he left 99 East right after their threesome dinner the night of the murder to go back to his own apartment. Is there any counter evidence connecting Ennis even indirectly with the actual crime?"

"Maybe."

"You've been holding out on me!"

"I shouldn't be telling you this at all. Suppose I told you," the Inspector said, "that we have a witness who saw Ennis drive away from in front of his brownstone shortly before 9 o'clock that night, and another witness who saw him come home around 3:30 in the morning?"

"Has Ennis been questioned about that?"

"Yes."

"What did he say?"

"He denied having left his place at any time after he got home that evening from the Impotunas' dinner. He said he watched television for a while and then went to bed. Everybody in on the interrogation agreed he was lying in his teeth. He's not a very convincing liar."

"How reliable are your witnesses?"

"The D.A. thinks so much of them he's ready to go for a grand jury indictment. Murder One."

Ellery was silent. Finally he said, "Conspiracy?"

"Yes."

"Not much of a case."

"In how many Murder Ones do you get an eyewitness?" The Inspector shrugged. "There's been all sorts of howls to lay this case to rest, Ellery. From the mountaintops. At that, it may turn out to be a better case than it looks. Those two were two-timing Importuna for a fact, so

205

they've got to have guilty consciences to start with. The D.A. thinks one of them may break."

"What about all those 9s?" Ellery murmured.

"They're the work of a nut. Or they're just red herrings. Either way they don't mean anything."

"What did you say?"

"What did I say about what?"

"Red herrings . . ."

"That's right. What's the matter with you?"

"Red herrings." Ellery's echo sounded fevered. His father stared at him. "You know, dad, you may have put your finger on the crux of this thing? That could be exactly what they are! Nothing more or less than red herrings."

"That's what I just said —"

"But could they all be red herrings?" Ellery muttered. "So many of them? Every *one* of them?" He sailed out of the cracked black leather chair that had been his by right of occupancy over years of similar consultations, and he began to semaphore with his long arms. "Did I ever quote you that 17th century nonsense rhyme written by everybody's favorite author, Anon.?

A man in the wilderness asked me,
How many strawberries grow in the sea?
I answered him, as I thought good,
As many as red herrings grow in the wood.

"Red herrings in the wood. The *forest.* Daddy, I do believe I've got something!"

"I'll tell you what you've got," his father grunted. "You've got sunstroke."

"No, listen —"

But at this juncture Sergeant Thomas Velie plunged through the Inspector's doorway holding aloft by its sharp edges a familiar-looking envelope.

"Would you believe it?" the sergeant shouted. "Another letter from Friend Nutsy. Special delivery this time."

"Impossible," Ellery said. "Impossible!"

But it was true. The message read:

WHO WAS WITH VIRGINIA LUNCH
DECEMBER NINE NINETEEN SIXTY-
    SIX?

"It's from the same crackpot," the Inspector said in disgust. "Same hand-printed capitals, same ball-point ink, same post-office stamped envelope —"

"And the same 9 words. Well, hardly the same," Ellery said rapidly. "You know, dad, this could be an interesting development. If your correspondent is a crackpot, he certainly seems to be a crackpot with inside information."

"You mean like Nino was a semipro ball-player, and had a golf course, and all those other interesting developments that developed to be opium dreams?"

"Just the same, I wonder whom Virginia did lunch with on December 9, 1966. Any information on that in the file?"

"I can't tell you where *I* was on December 9, 1966," his father said, exasperated. "How should I know where she was?"

"Then I suggest you find out."

"*You* find out. This bird's wasted enough of the city's money."

"Then it's all right if I go on a fishing trip vis-à-vis Virginia Importuna? While you mosey on over to the D.A.'s office and get him to hold off a bit on his great big prosecutional plans? Thanks, dad!"

Ellery dashed.

"What's on your mind this time, Mr. Queen." Then Virginia smiled a little. "I mean, I know what's on your mind — it's always the same thing, isn't it? — but there must be some new angle you're working on."

"It's not what I'm working on that should be concerning you, Mrs. Importuna," Ellery said in his most Delphic tones. "It's what the district attorney and Centre Street are working on."

The stunning eyes grew huge. "What do you mean?"

"I'm going to tell you something that could get me into a great deal of trouble if it became known downtown that I'd tipped you off, Mrs. Importuna. The D.A. is preparing at this moment to haul you before a grand jury with the hope of getting an indictment against you on a murder-conspiracy charge."

"Conspiracy . . ."

"You see, they know what's been going on behind your husband's back, Mrs. Importuna, between Peter Ennis and you."

She was quiet for so long that he began to think she had turned her ears off in shock. That, and her pallor, were the only signs of recoil from his thunderclap.

"Mrs. Importuna?"

A bit of pink came back to her cheeks. "Pardon me, I was thinking over my sinful life," she said. "I suppose I can't blame them for building up all sorts of wickednesses against me. But I didn't kill Nino, Mr. Queen, and that's the truth. I suppose it would be naïve of me to expect that you'd believe me."

"Oh, I don't know. I was born with a sort of openwork mind. Full of holes, as my detractors have been known to say." Ellery smiled at her. "But then I don't have the obligation of the authorities to produce results for various Pooh-Bahs, up to and including the biggest Pooh-Bah of them all, the public. So don't be too hard on the poor fellows. You must admit that the appearances, at least, favor the theory they're working on."

"Why are you telling me this, Mr. Queen?"

"Let's say I'm not satisfied with the official theory. I'm not satisfied at all, Mrs. Importuna. Oh, I don't doubt you and Peter have been having an affair — I'd decided that quite independently from the police. But I'm not convinced you could kill anyone in cold blood, and this was a coldblooded homicide. Of course, I could be dead wrong about you; I've been wrong before, and more than once. This time, though, I confess I'd like to be right."

"Thank you." Virginia's murmur held a glissando of surprise.

"Now as to why I'm here. Whether you answer my question or not depends on whether you decide to trust me or not. I hope you'll decide to trust me. On December 9th last, Mrs. Importuna, you had lunch with somebody. Who was it?"

She actually giggled. "What a freaky question after that buildup! Do you really expect me to remember something as trivial as a lunch date 10 months ago?"

"Try, please. It may turn out to be the reverse of trivial. It may, in fact, be vital to you."

His solemnity seemed to impress her. For some time her eyes went away, somewhere. Finally they came back to him. "I suppose I'm an idiot, but I've decided you're not trying to trick me." Ellery chose to remain quiet. "It happens that there is a way to answer your question, Mr. Queen. For a great many years I've kept a diary. I haven't missed a day since I was 14 years old. It's always been for me — I hope you won't laugh — an Emily Dickinson kind of thing to do. I was once absolutely convinced I was going to be the latter-day Emily, dressing only in white, and spending practically all my time in my room writing poems that would never die. . . . Well, you're not interested in my girlish dreams. But I do have a record of day-to-day events as they concerned me."

"Yes," Ellery said, "yes, that would certainly do it."

He rose as she rose. He was holding his breath.

"I'll be right back," Virginia said.

She was gone for a century.

When she returned it was with an oversize diary in gold-tooled black morocco leather. It had a latch-flap-lock arrangement. Ellery had to command himself like a squad leader to keep from grabbing.

"This is my diary for 1966."

"That's the one, yes."

"Do sit down again, Mr. Queen."

She sank onto her sofa, a Duncan Phyfe, he thought, from its lyre motif; and he seated himself opposite her, trying to concentrate on the sofa to avoid being caught coveting the diary. She turned a gold key in the lock. The little key was on a gold chain.

"Let's see, now. December what did you say, Mr. Queen?"

"The 9th."

"9th, 9th . . . Here it is . . . Oh," she said. "*That* day."

"Yes?" Ellery said lightly. "Something special about that day, Mrs. Importuna?"

"You might say so! It was the first time I had that naughty thing the Victorians used to call a tryst with Peter. A public one, at that. I seem to recall Nino was off in Europe or somewhere on business. It was a stupidly dangerous thing for us to do, but it was a little hideaway place nobody I knew patronized. . . ."

He almost said, May I have a look at that, Mrs. Importuna? but he stopped himself on the cliff edge of importunity, aware how vulnerable she must be feeling, wondering how she had dared even to admit the existence of her diary, let alone produce it. Its contents in the wrong hands . . . His hands?

To his stupefaction he heard her say, "But why tell you about it, Mr. Queen? Read it for yourself."

And there it was, being placed in his hands.

"Mrs. Importuna," Ellery said. "Do you realize what you're proposing to do? You're offering me information that, if it turns out to be pertinent, I'm in conscience bound to pass along to my father. My father is one of the officers investigating this case. The only reason I'm given the run of these premises by the officers on duty downstairs is because of my father. And, in any event, I shan't be able to prevent your being charged and arraigned — or in all probability even to delay matters. Do you understand that?"

"Yes."

"And you're still willing to let me read your entry for the day in question?"

There were delicate little butterfly bruises of worry and tension under her eyes. But the eyes themselves were unclouded.

"I didn't kill my husband, Mr. Queen. I didn't plot with anyone to kill him. I did fall in love with Peter Ennis, who's a kind as well as a beautiful man. But since you already know we're in love, how can my diary hurt us?"

He opened it gently.

And read:

December 9, 1966. I wonder why I keep adding to this, oh, *construction*. This higgledy-piggledy, slam-bang architecture of feelings . . . hopes, disappointments, terrors, joys, the lot. Is it because of the joys? The few I have? And the almost addictive need to express them? Then why do I keep dwelling on the bad scenes? Sometimes I think this isn't worth the risk. If N. were ever to find you, Diary . . .

He read on, immersing himself in the flow of her thoughts and feelings, analyzing her narrative of that day's events — her meeting with Ennis in the little undistinguished restaurant, Peter's hammering away at her to divorce Nino Importuna . . . all the way through her dread of what "I glimpsed in Peter's eyes . . . and if his parting shot to me meant what I think it meant, the embryo's going to turn out to be a thalidomide baby, or worse." And her final, unsteady "and to hell with you and you and you too Mrs. Calabash. I'd better totter off and tucky my lil ole self into beddy-snooky-bye."

213

He shut the leather-covered book and handed it back. Virginia inserted the key in the lock and turned the key, slipped its chain about her neck, dropped the key into the chasm between her breasts.

The diary, locked, lay in her lap.

"Do you mind if we don't talk for a while?"

Ellery rose without waiting for a response and began to stroll about, rubbing the back of his neck, fingering his ear, pulling at his nose, finally resting his forehead against the edge of the tall mantelpiece at the fireplace. Virginia's eyes followed him. She seemed to have resigned herself to whatever fate had reserved for her, and to be waiting for it in confident patience. After some time this aura of self-confidence reached Ellery and penetrated his field of concentration. He came back from the fireplace and looked down at her.

"Where do you hide your diaries, Mrs. Importuna?"

"In a very safe place," Virginia replied. "Don't ask me where, because I won't tell you."

"Does anyone know the hiding place?"

"Not a soul in this world." She added, "Or the next."

"Not even Peter Ennis?"

"I just said, Mr. Queen, no one."

"There's no possibility someone could have got his hands on this particular volume and read it?"

"No possibility. That I'd stake my life on."

She smiled. "Or is that what I'm doing, Mr. Queen? No. There's only one master key to all the years, the one you just saw me use, and I keep the chain around my neck always, even when I bathe. Even when I sleep."

"Your husband. Couldn't he have . . . ?"

"I never slept with my husband," Virginia said in a murderous voice. "Never! When he was finished with me I invariably went back to my own room. And locked the filthy door."

"Mrs. Importuna, I must ask you something —"

"Don't."

"Forgive me. Was Importuna fond of the use of a whip?"

She shut her eyes as if to seek forgetfulness in the dark. But she opened them almost at once.

"The answer to that happens to be no. But if what you want to know is what he *was* fond of, don't bother to ask the question. I won't answer it. No one — no one, Mr. Queen — will ever know that from me. And the only other one who could tell is dead."

Ellery took her hand; it lay in his trustfully, like a child's. "You're a very remarkable lady," he said. "I'm in great danger of falling in love with you." But then he let go of her hand and his tone changed. "I don't know yet how this is all going to turn out. However it does, you haven't seen the last of me."

He was the perfect nonentity, a Chesterton's

postman of a somewhat higher order.

Mr. E was neither tall nor short, fat nor thin, blond nor brunet, young nor old, shag-haired nor bald. His face might have been made of dough, or Plasticine. It possessed the property of accommodating itself to his immediate environment, so that he became part of it, like a face in a crowd.

He was dressed, not sharply and not shabbily, in a suit of neutral gray showing signs of wear hardly — indeed, just — noticeable; under the jacket he had on a not quite new white shirt and a medium shade of gray necktie with tiny darker gray figures; on his feet were black English brogues with a dull shine, worn down a bit at the heels.

He grasped a dark gray fedora in one hand and a well-used black attaché case in the other.

His obvious specialty, the only obvious thing about him, was self-effacement. Not the most knowing eye would ordinarily give him a second glance.

This was not an ordinary occasion, however, and Inspector Queen looked Mr. E over with the closest attention to detail. Nino Importuna's confidential agent had been accompanied to Centre Street by two detectives of the Inspector's staff; they had picked him up deplaning from an El Al jet at Kennedy. He stood up under the Inspector's scrutiny with patience and equanimity, but also as if modestly aware of his worth; and he sat down at the Inspector's invitation in an unobtrusive way, so that one moment he was on his feet and the next he was seated in the chair, leaving no recollection behind of how he had accomplished the transition. His neat hands were clasped on the attaché case in his lap.

And he waited.

"You're known at 99 East as Mr. E," Inspector Queen began. "You traveled — on this last trip, anyway — under a cover name, Kempinski, and your real name, we've now found out, is Edward Lloyd Merkenthaler. What do I call you?"

"Take your choice." Mr. E had a mild, soft voice, rather like a lady's bath suds; it seemed to vanish discreetly down a drain the moment he produced it. If he was disturbed at having been taken off a plane by two New York City detectives and brought to Police Headquarters for questioning in a homicide he showed no sign of it. "In my business I've found it more convenient to use many names, Inspector. I don't have a preference."

"Well, I do. So let's use your real name. Mr. Merkenthaler, do you have any objections to answering some questions?"

"None at all."

"Do you know your rights?"

"Oh, yes."

"Would you rather have a lawyer present?"

Mr. E's lips rose in an appreciative smile, as if the Inspector had granted him a witticism. "That won't be at all necessary."

"A moment ago you mentioned your business. Exactly what is your business, Mr. Merkenthaler?"

"For a number of years I've been employed by Nino Importuna — not by Importuna Industries; Mr. Importuna paid me out of his personal funds — as what might be called a peripatetic industrial detective, or a white-collar prospector, or both."

"Meaning what?"

"I tracked down businesses Mr. Importuna was interested in absorbing, investigating them for soundness and commercial possibilities, that sort of thing. Or I hunted up new prospects for him. I hold graduate degrees in engineering, geology, and business administration and finance, among others. It's been largely on my recommendations that Mr. Importuna bought most of his properties."

"Why all the mumbo jumbo and cloak-and-dagger stuff?"

"You mean the reason for the secrecy and anonymity, Inspector? Well, once it were to become known that Nino Importuna was after a property, there would be all sorts of opportunities for fraud and chicanery and doctoring of books; and even if not, the price was sure to be jacked up. It produced quicker and better results for me to operate under a cover for unnamed parties."

"You said you've been employed in this confidential work for Importuna for a number of years," Inspector Queen said suddenly. "The number wouldn't be 9, would it?"

Mr. E elevated his brows. "I see you know about his superstition. No, Inspector, it's been closer to 15."

The Inspector reddened, and his tone grew sharper than he intended. "We got your cable just a few hours ago. Where've you been all these weeks? Importuna's death made headlines all over the world. How come you didn't get in touch with someone at Importuna Industries long before this?"

"I didn't know Mr. Importuna was dead until my flight landed in Rome last night. I hadn't seen a newspaper or a newscast or listened to the radio since early in September."

"That's pretty hard to believe, Mr. Merkenthaler."

"Not really, when you know the circumstances," Mr. E responded amiably. "I've been critically ill in a Tel Aviv hospital, to which I was brought in a state of unconsciousness from deep in the Negev — a business matter I'm not at liberty to disclose at least until I've had a chance to report to whoever's in charge now at 99 East, I suppose Mrs. Importuna. Lobar streptococcal pneumonia, involving both lungs. And complications set in. The Israeli doctors told me later that twice they gave me up for dead. Before the antibiotics, they said, I wouldn't have had a chance."

"This will all be checked out, of course."

Mr. E seemed titillated. "Am I to understand that you're considering me a suspect in the murder of Nino Importuna?"

"Where were you, Mr. Merkenthaler, on the night of September 9th, around midnight?"

"Ah. Excuse me." The industrial agent produced a key with a sly flourish, like a magician, and unlocked his attaché case. He raised the lid a very little way, as if reluctant to expose its contents to the eyes of strangers. From the case he took a 5-in-1-type traveler's memorandum book, shut the case at once, and leafed through the book.

"I assume, Inspector Queen, when you say the night of September 9th you're referring to the date and time in New York City?"

The Inspector looked puzzled. "Yes?"

"Well, it makes a difference, you know, when you're on the other side of the planet. Midnight on September 9th in New York City would be Eastern Daylight Saving Time. But when it was midnight of September 9th EDST in the United States I happened to be in Israel on business. Israel is seven hours later than New York in terms of standard times. I believe Israel's on standard time; traveling as much as I do, it's not easy to keep track of time differences the world over, and especially time manipulations. At any rate, whichever it is, you want to know where I was between, say, six and seven hours past New York EDST on midnight September 9th, or in other words between 6 and 7 A.M. Israeli time on September 10th.

"At that hour, Inspector Queen," Mr. E went

on, tapping his memorandum book, "it's noted here that I was aboard a private airplane owned by the Menachem-Lipsky-Negev Development Company, Ltd., en route to a certain location in the desert. I can't disclose the whereabouts of the site or really anything about the project; I gave my word I would keep our negotiations in the strictest confidence, and my business, Inspector, rests on the integrity of my word.

"At any rate, I came down ill immediately on landing in the desert and I was flown back to hospital in Tel Aviv that same morning, running a temperature, they said afterward, of over 106°. The company and hospital authorities will, of course, corroborate my statement.

"Do you want the cable address or telephone number of the Menachem-Lipsky-Negev Development Company, and the names of the pilot, the employees who met me in the desert, and the doctors in Tel Aviv who saved my life? And oh, yes," Mr. E added shyly. "When you check my story, be sure to inquire about me under the name of Mortimer C. Ginsberg. Otherwise they won't know whom you're talking about."

November 9, 1967

Ellery selected the date and site of the confrontation to satisfy the esthetics of the case and the yearning for justice in his heart: the 9th of the month and Nino Importuna's bedroom, where the industrialist had met his death.

Inspector Queen consented with misgivings; he insisted on having a member of the district attorney's staff present.

"What can go wrong?" Ellery had said with none of his customary humility; he was positively euphoric. "You know me, dad. I've had a really hard time, but I've finally run it down. I never pull a drawstring till I know my quarry's in the bag."

"Sure, son, sure," his father had said through the gnawed-ragged fringe of his mustache. "But just supposing, I want to be covered."

"Have you no faith?"

"This case has made an agnostic out of me!"

The assistant D.A. was a young man named Rankin whom Ellery did not know. The lawyer stationed himself in a corner of the room, from where he had a panoramic view of the action. The expression on his foxy face said that, while he hoped for the best out of this unheard-of, if not illegal, proceeding, all he could realistically look forward to was the reverse. Ellery ignored him.

The only others present, aside from the Queens, were Virginia Importuna and Peter Ennis. The widow was almost serenely expectant; she might have been taking her seat at an opening night. Ennis, however, was pallidly twitchy, a very nervous young man. Ellery smiled at both of them.

"The secret of this offbeat case," he began, "lies in its 9s. All along I've been convinced that the 9s in Nino Importuna's murder constituted the crucial element — that if only we could fathom their real meaning we'd reach the treasure. But it remained unfound until you, dad, inadvertently provided the key. You referred to the 9s as red herrings.

"Those words unlocked the door.

"The 9s lying in heaps around the corpus of the case," Ellery went on — "were some of them contrived? Deliberately invented? Red herring used to be used in training tracking dogs; the strong smell of smoked fish tended to throw them off the scent. Did the 9s in the Importuna case serve an analogous purpose?

"I explored the hypothesis. Assuming they did, which of the 9s had been dragged across the trail to make the job of tracking down the killer harder, if not impossible?"

The assistant D.A. began to look interested. He dug out a pad and pencil.

"I didn't really get anywhere on this tack until

I recalled G. K. Chesterton's 'The Sign of the Broken Sword,' one of the short stories in *The Innocence of Father Brown*. At one point in this story Father Brown asks the reformed thief, Flambeau, 'Where does a wise man hide a pebble?' Flambeau answers, 'On the beach.' 'Where,' Father Brown goes on, 'does a wise man hide a leaf?' Flambeau replies, 'In the forest.' At which Flambeau asks, 'Do you mean that when a wise man has to hide a real diamond he has been known to hide it among sham ones?'

"This recollection furnished me with the key question I was groping for. I paraphrased Flambeau: 'Do you mean that when a murderer has to hide a real clue he might hide it among sham ones?'

"I immediately saw the murderer's dilemma plain and his plan clear: There was a genuine 9-clue which pointed to him as the guilty party and which he could not wish out of existence. At the same time he could not afford, in self-defense, to leave it as it was. Therefore he would hide it, like Father Brown's pebble, on a beach of 9-clues, all but one of which were false. In the confusion the only significant one, the legitimate one, would go unnoticed. At least, that was his thinking and his objective. In any event, he had nothing to lose and a great deal to gain — his safety — by drawing his red herrings across the trail.

"The obvious counterploy was to check back on all the 9s, to take them one by one out of the net and see which were herrings. We came up with a strange catch."

Ellery turned to Virginia Importuna.

"Your husband's totem, the number 9, has its apparent inception in the date he claimed for his birth, September 9, 1899. I proceeded to question its validity, as I meant to question all the 9s in the case, by procuring a copy through an Italian inquiry agency of Importuna's baptismal certificate. Sure enough, it turned out that he was born not in 1899 but in the year before, and not in the 9th month of that year but in the fifth, and not on the 9th day of that month but on the 16th. May 16, 1898 was a far cry from September 9, 1899; as a 9 totem, it failed completely. So he simply appropriated as his birth date the 9th day of the 9th month in the year that added up to 9 every which way.

"In other words, the 9s in his professed birth date were, as Chesterton put it, a sham, satisfying not the truth but your husband's superstition. A red herring.

"His name, Importuna, composed of 9 letters? Sham: His real name was Importunato, 11 letters. His Christian name, Nino, its number values adding up to 9? Sham: His real Christian name was Tullio. The whole name Nino Importuna was a red herring.

"This building, 99 East. My father had it checked. And found that 99 was not its original street number. Originally it was 97; there was no number 99 on this street. To satisfy his need for surrounding himself with 9s, Importuna had the building renumbered 99 when he bought it; with his means and power it was no problem. And 9 floors? A more subtle sham. A 9-story building with a penthouse apartment can more properly be said to have, not 9 floors, but 10."

"I didn't know about Nino's real birth date, Mr. Queen, or the renumbering of the building," Virginia said. "Did you, Peter?"

Ennis started at being addressed and quickly removed from his mouth the knuckle he was gnawing on. "They're both news to me."

"But these were not the important red herrings," Ellery said. "Let's dip into our net again.

"The time of death: Your husband's wristwatch, Mrs. Importuna, stopped by a blow, fixed the time of the murder attack at 9 minutes past 9 o'clock. Sham: The medical examiner placed death at shortly past midnight, about three hours later than the stopped watch indicated. The murderer must have set the watch back after the killing and then struck it to stop it, thereby giving us the 9th minute past the 9th hour of the evening, and two more red herrings to chew on. And, by the way, the M.E.'s postmortem report even exposed the date of death — September 9th — as a sham. A few minutes after midnight put the actual date of death at the next day, September 10th.

"Now consider in this context the weapon used, that curvy abstraction in cast iron we — especially I — were so eager to see as a 9-shape, when the killer went out of his way to get hold of it for the commission of his crime. Can there be any doubt that its resemblance to a 9 was his reason for choosing it? Yet it's really not a 9. To the sculptor, according to the title he gave it, it was *Newborn Child Emerging.*"

"But it does look like a 9," Peter protested.

"Held in one position, yes. But turn it upside down — how can you ever be sure with an abstraction? — and it becomes a 6. Sham. Red herring.

"And again. The number of the killer's blows with the sculpture as his not-so-blunt instrument. We kept saying he struck 9 blows. We were wrong. The killer struck 10 blows. The blow to the wrist, to stop the watch at the phony time, according to Dr. Prouty was not a glance-off from one of the 9 blows to the head but a separate blow, in his opinion not even delivered by the same weapon. Red herring again."

Inspector Queen muttered, "There were lots more 9s," and then he looked about him guiltily.

"It's all right, dad, there's no point in still keeping it a secret. So we come to the anonymous letters, with their contents."

"Hold on there, Queen!" the assistant D.A. said. He was standing behind Virginia and Peter, and he jabbed his forefingers meaningly in their direction.

"I said it's all right, Mr. Rankin. I should explain," Ellery continued, turning to Virginia and Peter, "that my father was in receipt of a series of anonymous messages at Police Head-quarters which were kept secret from all but a handful of officials."

"Now you've tied it," Rankin said angrily. "I was against this from the start, and I told the D.A. so!"

Ellery paid no attention to him.

"Some of the envelopes from the killer — the 9-significance of some of the messages made it obvious that they were sent by the Importuna killer — some of them contained playing cards, one whole card or one-half card to a message. Clearly they were intended to convey a meaning. Meanings are conveyed by playing cards, of course, in fortune-telling. I chose to interpret the cards according to a popular fortune-telling system. But the fact is there are a number of fortune-telling systems, in each of which individual cards can have entirely different meanings. The sender of the cards never specified or even hinted at which interpretive system was to be used. So the meanings I ascribed to them were purely arbitrary and for that reason not necessarily relevant. Red herrings, like the zip code numbers of the post offices he picked to mail the envelopes from, which added up to 9s.

"Even the quantity of messages was a sham. True, 9 were received. But then a 10th arrived, compromising the magic number. Red herrings.

"In five of the envelopes there were verbal messages. One stated that a boyhood friend of Importuna's had grown up to become a justice

228

of the Supreme Court. The 9-significance of the United States Supreme Court is known to every schoolchild. The trouble was, an exhaustive inquiry failed to turn up such a boyhood friend — or any such friend — of Nino's. The message was simply false. Or, in Chesterton's word, sham. In your words, dad, red herring.

"The same proved true of the other four worded messages. One stated that in his youth Nino Importuna had played semiprofessional baseball for the Binghamton, New York, team. Only it wasn't so. Another said that his Palm Springs estate included a golf course — another connotation of 9, from either a 9-hole course or an 18-hole, a multiple of 9. Only neither proved to be true. There was no golf course at all on the Importuna Palm Spring property.

"Another message — forgive me for mentioning it, Mrs. Importuna — alleged Importuna's fondness for a cat-o'-nine-tails. Mrs. Importuna assured me that it wasn't true, and no evidence of any sexual aberration could be found.

"Then there was the message about Impotuna's having commissioned the sculpturing of the 9 Muses for his villa in Lugano. You, Peter, emphatically denied this, telling me it was just the sort of assignment it was your job to oversee, yet you knew nothing about any such commission. There would have been no point in your lying about it, because the simplest investigation would turn up the sculptor of such a project if the message were telling the truth. The official investigation, in fact, found no trace of such a person.

"So the 9 messages were either irrelevant or false. I was trying to eliminate the sham clues, remember, to discover which 9-clue was *not* a sham, was *not* a red herring. And here I was faced with the dismaying conclusion that *all* the 9s were red herrings! — certainly all that had the least smack of importance. Nino could sign contracts on the 9th, the 18th, or the 27th of the month, or refuse to close a deal except on such dates, or arrange to be married on the 9th day of the 9th month for luck, or falsify his birth date to make it drip 9s, but the 9-isms like these were not really clues. They were things that Impotuna, not his killer, had elected to do. I had set out to find a legitimate 9-ism relating to the killer, and here I was with nothing left in the net. Until suddenly that was no longer true. I had eliminated every 9-clue, I then saw," Ellery said, "except one."

This was the climax of his carefully plotted scene, and Ellery played it as he had played similar scenes at similar climaxes, holding them with a glittering eye, using his voice as if it were a foil, dominating them with his presence, threatening them with a stabbing forefinger.

"*Except one,*" he repeated. "One 9 was real. One 9 was *not* a red herring.

"It was the last 9-ism of the series, emerging as a result of message number 10.

"This unexpected, 9-total-breaking final message, Mrs. Importuna, was the basis of the question I asked you about your luncheon date with Peter Ennis on December 9, 1966." Virginia flinched, then braced herself with a scornful look. "I'm sorry, but I have no choice. I told you that I couldn't promise to keep your diary in confidence from the authorities if I found it contained information pertinent to the case."

"Information? What information?" Inspector Queen was bristling. And Assistant District Attorney Rankin was jotting away at a tremendous pace.

"Mrs. Importuna has kept a diary from girlhood, dad. She was kind enough to let me read her entry for December 9, 1966. From that entry I learned that in the course of her lunch that day — it was with Ennis — a 9-ism cropped up. It was this." Ellery leaned forward. "That Virginia's and Nino's prenuptial agreement had exactly 9 more months to run — 9 months from that day, December 9, 1966, to September 9, 1967, which was the cutoff date specified in the agreement for Mrs. Importuna to become her husband's sole heir."

"Now that 9-month-to-the-day period was no invention of somebody's, no sham, no red herring. That 9 months was a fact. And it was a significant fact. Because if someone wanted Virginia to inherit her husband's half-billion-dollar estate, he *had* to wait 9 months before her claim to it became a legal, if potential, reality.

"In a grimly real sense this whole unavoidable

9-month waiting period resembles a pregnancy. Conception occurs on December 9, 1966. There are 9 months of gestation. Then on September 9, 1967, the child is born, the monstrous child, and its name is murder. Why, even the forceps used in its delivery bears the label *Newborn Child Emerging.*"

Ellery paused for breath, and they hitched forward, even Rankin in his corner, to urge him on.

"Let's consider the occasion of what I've called the conception, that lunch in a hideaway restaurant on December 9th of last year. I was looking for a clue, remember, that in some way involved the killer. I had to ask myself, was there anything about that lunch the killer might have reason to dread? Well, *what about the fact of the meeting itself?* Suppose Virginia's and Peter's appearance in public, their only indiscretion as far as the outside world was concerned, were to become known? Suppose they had been seen and their conversation overheard? For if it became known that Virginia Importuna and Peter Ennis, her husband's confidential secretary, were having an affair, if it became known that because of her prenuptial agreement Virginia couldn't leave or divorce her husband without losing everything, if it became known that Peter had to wait 9 months for Virginia to become Importuna's heir — from these simple facts all the rest . . . the conception of Impotuna's murder, the gestation of the murder plot, and the birth, the fruition, of the crime . . . could

232

be deduced by anyone with an IQ of 100. And that was a mortal danger to the plotter. That was the 9-fact he tried to bury in that barrage of sham 9s he bombarded us with after the murder was born."

Inspector Queen had begun to develop a pinched and greenish expression about the mouth, as if he were trying without success to ignore an extremely bad taste.

"To wrap this up," Ellery continued with an encouraging smile at his father — Courage! Fear not! — "let me explain what I mean by the period of gestation. The plotter, as I said, had to wait 9 months before Virginia could come into Importuna's estate, after which he would kill Importuna. Why not use that 9-month waiting period to the best possible advantage? After all, on December 9th of last year Nino Importuna owned only a third of the family fortune. But if Nino's two brothers were to die in the meantime . . . So he murdered Julio and framed Marco for it, thus counting on being rid of both.

"The frame-up wasn't quite successful, but Marco was so obliging as to commit suicide, the police concluded that this constituted in effect a confession that Marco had killed Julio and hanged himself in remorse; the net effect to the plotter was perfectly satisfactory. Both younger brothers were dead, he — the plotter-killer — was unsuspected, and Nino's fortune was tripled. So that when that September day rolled around on which Virginia became Nino's legal heir, the final act — the killing of Nino — would bring the killer a half-billion-dollar fortune. Not directly, of course, but through his tie with you, Virginia. Because I'm positive you and he have long since made plans to marry —"

"Not directly? Marry?" Peter Ennis was on his feet, looking suddenly formidable.

"What in hell are you hinting at, Queen?"

Ellery frowned. Virginia was smiling.

"If you'll allow me to finish, Peter," he said, "you'll find it's rather more than a hint."

"You don't have to hint, old boy. What you're doing or are about to do is accuse me of having plotted to kill Virginia's husband beginning 9 months before the actual murder and, during those 9 months, of having got rid of Julio and Marco in order to triple Virginia's inheritance when she should come into it. Right? And I'm supposed to have done all this in the expectation of marrying her and so getting control of the Importuna fortune?"

"Very well put, Peter," Ellery said. "That's just what I'm accusing you of."

Peter grinned. He glanced at Virginia, whose smile became a tittery sort of giggle.

"I'm sorry, Mr. Queen," she said, "this is so rude of me. And you *are* doing your best."

"What do you mean?" Ellery demanded, reddening. "Have I said something funny?"

"You sure have," Peter said. "Hilarious. I take it if I can prove I couldn't have killed Nino Importuna I'm off your stupid hook?"

"Peter, now, really," Virginia chided him. "That's not a nice way to talk to Mr. Queen. I'm sure he's done the very best anyone could expect."

"So did the snake in the Garden of Eden! I don't exactly enjoy being suspected of murder, darlin'. Well, Queen, do you want the proof?"

"Of course." Ellery was standing there looking like a small boy who has just awakened from a delicious dream to find himself soaked to the skin.

"Inspector Queen, when exactly was Nino murdered?" Peter Ennis demanded. "Lay it out for us again. What time of night?"

"Just past midnight of September 9th–10th." The Inspector avoided Ellery's piteous glance. "About 12:15 A.M. of, technically, the 10th of September."

"Be sure to take this all down, Mr. Rankin. It's the stopper to that arrest order you've probably got burning a hole in your pocket.

"Nino Importuna, Virginia, and I had dinner together in the penthouse that evening — the evening of the 9th — as we told you people long ago. Toward the end of the dinner Nino complained of not feeling well, as you know, and he went to his room after telling us to eat the chef's special dessert without him. Virginia and I did so, and I immediately left. What I didn't testify to was that when I drove to my apartment I changed my clothes, threw a toothbrush and pajamas into my briefcase, and drove back to the

235

vicinity of 99 East. Virginia was waiting for me at our prearranged spot —"

"How did she do that without being seen leaving the building?" Ellery jeered.

"Let me, Peter," Virginia said, "since it's me Mr. Queen's talking about. It was really quite simple, Mr. Queen. The building next door is flush against ours, and just one story lower. There's a steel ladder on our roof that can be lowered to theirs in an emergency. I'd purposely dressed in a dark slack suit. I lowered the ladder, climbed down to the other roof, got into their elevator, which is self-service, and simply rode down to the street. They don't have a night doorman or a security guard. I got back to the penthouse later the same way, just pulling the ladder back up when I was on our roof."

Ellery sat down on Importuna's bed. It was less a sitting down than collapse.

Peter Ennis said with some satisfaction, "We drove up to Connecticut — New Milford, Queen. Registered there in a motel under the names of Mr. and Mrs. Michael Angelo — Virginia thought that sounded romantic. The trip up took two hours of fast driving — I don't see how anyone could make it in less time in a car. We checked into the motel just about 11 P.M. — their records should show the time to the minute, because they use a time-and-dating machine on the slips. Even if we'd left the place immediately and driven back to the city, we couldn't possibly have reached 99 East before 1 A.M., which would have made it almost an hour after Nino was murdered. As it is, we didn't actually check out until around 1:30 A.M. — you'll find the exact time recorded up there. I dropped Virginia off at the building next door at 3:30 A.M. and drove on to my apartment.

"I should make the point, I suppose," Peter went on, looking them in the eyes, "that the reason we didn't tell the truth about that night until you just made it impossible for us not to, Queen, was that we didn't expect anyone really to understand how much we've been in love for so long, that it's been the real thing for both of us, that we couldn't face having it cheapened further — it was cheapened enough in our own eyes by the circumstances.

"Now that I've said it," Peter said, "you'll want to know the name of the motel —"

"We know the name of the motel," Inspector Queen said. "It's been checked out, Ellery — not only the registration and departure times, but also positive IDs of Ennis and Mrs. Importuna from photos we showed the night clerk who saw them come and go. I didn't get the chance to tell you, son, in the rush today."

"But you must have known what I had in mind when I set this up, dad," Ellery said wildly. He was clutching the edge of Importuna's bed with both hands as if it were the edge of a precipice.

"Not really, son. You were pretty mysterious about what you had in mind. I thought you'd be pulling the rabbit out of your hat as usual, one of your magic tricks that turn a case upside down the way you've done so often. Ellery, if you can't disprove the alibi, these people are in the clear. And you can't. Why do you think those subpoenas weren't served? On the evidence, neither Mrs. Importuna nor Ennis could physically have been here at the time Importuna was attacked and murdered."

"I'm sorry, Mr. Queen, I really am," Virginia murmured again, as if she would happily have confessed to the crime if only to save Ellery from further embarrassment. "I'm sure you'll figure out the real answer one of these days."

Mercifully, Ellery was not listening. He was mumbling to himself. He was mumbling, "Those 9s. Those damn 9s. They've got to be the key to this nightmare. But what?"

"Where you went wrong, son," the Inspector said later that night, over Ellery's favorite pastrami sandwiches and celery tonic from the kosher delicatessen around the corner, "was in not spotting the big hole in your argument."

"Hole?" He was chewing away at the Rumanian delicacy, but only out of respect for tradition. "What hole?"

"If Peter Ennis had been the killer, then he sent that final anonymous letter, number 10. But if he was the guilty party that's the last thing he'd have done. The message instructed us to find out who'd had lunch with Virginia on that certain date . . . the date that, according to you, began the 9-month waiting period till Virginia could come into Importuna's estate. Well, that's the one thing the killer couldn't possibly have wanted us to find out — the one thing he was trying his damnedest to hide by throwing all those 9s at us! You didn't think it through far enough, Ellery. As I said, about the only one in the world who *wouldn't* have sent that 10th message was Peter Ennis, if he'd been guilty."

"You're right, you're right," Ellery muttered. "How could I have made a slip like that? It's ridiculous. . . . But dad, there's something Virginia recorded Peter as having said to her that afternoon — I think while he was putting her into a cab right after lunch — something that's stuck in my craw ever since she let me read her diary."

"What was that?"

"She wrote that he said, 'There's only one thing for me to do and, by God, when the time is ripe I'm going to do it.' Certainly Virginia made no bones about what she thought Peter meant. And I interpreted it the same way: That when the 9 months were up and Virgina's inheritance was safely hers by will or however, Peter was going to put Importuna out of the way."

"Son, all that young fellow probably meant was that one of those days he was going to screw up his courage and have a talk with the old guy — stand up like a man to the hubby of the woman he loved and admit what had been going on, and try to convince him to give Virginia her

239

freedom. She let her imagination run away with her, and so did you."

Ellery made a face, as if he had found a German roach scuttling across his plate. It was not impossible, even the best of New York apartments being what they were, although in this case it happened not to be so.

He set the unfinished pastrami sandwich on the plate and said, "I don't know what I'm eating this for. I'm not hungry. I'll clean up, dad."

The sandwich, like his theory, wound up in the garbage.

December 9, 1967

Whether Virginia Importuna's predicted "one of these days" — when it came to pass and turned out to be the 9th day of the following month — was a satire of circumstance or a sly choice of Ellery's unconscious is a mystery he did not solve and never felt the urge to. However it came about, that Saturday was December 9. He tried very hard to forget the date the moment he became aware of it.

The intervening month since the debacle in Nino Importuna's bedroom had been a test, if not a positive trial, of his character. He could recall other failures among the happier memories of his past, one or two at least as painful; but this one seemed blended of a curious emotional mishmash of shame, self-disgust, and apprehension about his possibly waning faculties that, he suspected, derived as much from the fool it had made him appear in the eyes of a beautiful and delectable woman as from its own ingredients.

But he had survived it; he had even managed to leave it behind him by plunging into an 18-hour-a-day regimen on his neglected novel and, to his absolute amazement (and that of his publisher and agent), finishing it. Along the way, by a mysterious process which he could only

241

view as alchemical, he solved the Importuna-Importunato case.

At first, not unnaturally under the circumstances, he sniffed about the edges of his new solution like a suspicious cat; he could still taste the bitterness of the old one. But at last he was satisfied; and he made a telephone call, identified himself, and arranged an appointment for that afternoon with the murderer.

Who admitted him with the equanimity Ellery had expected.

"Will you have a drink, Mr. Queen?"

"Hardly," Ellery said. "For all I know you have a bottle of everything prepoisoned in anticipation of just such an occasion."

"In case you have a tape recorder hidden on you," the murderer responded with a smile — "sit down, Mr. Queen, my chairs at least are perfectly safe — I've never poisoned anyone in my life."

"With people like you there's always a first time," Ellery said, not smiling back. "You're sure this chair isn't electrified? Well, I suppose that would be pretty far out even for you."

He sat down, and rather to his relief nothing happened. "What am I supposed to have done, Mr. Queen? Not that I give a damn what you have to say; it can only be theory, not proof. But I confess — no, no, Queen, don't look so pathetically hopeful — I confess I'm curious."

"Oh, I imagine once the police know whom and what to look for," Ellery said, "the proof may come more easily than you think. Anyway, Sam Johnson once said that conjecture as to things useful is good, and could anything be of greater use to this world than putting you out of it?"

"You'll pardon me if I register a vigorous dissent. You won't think me rude if I drink alone, will you?" the murderer said, and poured a generous portion of Scotch over some ice cubes. "Now proceed, Queen. Amuse me."

"I can't promise to keep you in stitches," Ellery said, "although I hope to give you a tremor or two." And he related the theory he had expounded a month before in Nino Importuna's bedroom, and how the New Milford motel alibi had cleared Peter Ennis and Virginia Importuna and destroyed his lovely solution. "On the other hand, I wasn't going to let it drop there," Ellery continued. "I carry the invincible stubbornness of the Irish in my genes. My mind kept worrying it, and finally I got it."

"Got what?"

"The clue I'd missed."

"Nonsense," the murderer said. "There was no clue."

"Oh, but there was. It was there, plain as anything. So obvious, in fact, that I missed it the first time round. It was in Virginia's diary, in the account of her lunch with Peter that 9th of December a year ago — by the way, a year ago to the day. There's prophetic justice for you. You knew Virginia kept a diary, of course?"

"Of course."

"But she never allowed anyone to read it, and if you were ever tempted to do so without her permission you couldn't find it — she assured me that she kept her many volumes securely hidden. So you couldn't have known what Virginia noted in her long entry for that day, I mean the details, among which was the clue I mentioned. In that sense you were guilty of no blunder — I can't fault you for something you weren't aware of and couldn't have foreseen. You're a clever adversary indeed. One of the cleverest in my experience."

"Flattery will get you nowhere, Queen," the murderer said. "Gallop along on your fairy tale."

"If it is, it's a good deal grimmer than Grimm. Everything that I argued Peter had done was actually done by you. You, not Peter, were the one who had to wait 9 months for Virginia to become her husband's heir. You, not Peter, were the one who saw that by eliminating Nino's two brothers the fortune Virginia would be coming into would be tripled. So it was you, not Peter, who killed Julio and framed Marco for it.

"I can't prove evidentially that you planted that gold button from Marco's yachting jacket on the floor of Julio's study — it could conceivably have slipped through the hole in his pocket by sheer chance, but I'm always leery of happy accidents that just happen to coincide with a killer's interests, and I'm perfectly certain you did plant the button. And the shoeprint. And carefully arranged the signs of a struggle in the

244

study. And yes, shifted Julio's desk about for the reasons I gave at the time of the original investigation, which I shan't bother to repeat.

"The way it appears to me, what happened was this (I'm tempted to say, Correct me if I'm wrong, but I have the feeling you won't): you had the frame-up of Marco planned to the last detail — the planting of his button and his readily identifiable shoeprint in the cigar ashes from the deliberately upset ashtray; and, of course, the left-handed blow with the poker. You planned the left-handed assault on Julio frontally, across his desk, at which he was seated facing you. Unfortunately for the best-laid plans, just as you were about to bring the poker crashing down on target, Julio, in an instinctive attempt to dodge the blow, spun around in the swivel chair a full 180°, so that the *back* of his head was to you at the instant of impact, the descending poker landing on exactly the opposite side of his head from the side you'd aimed at to indicate left-handedness.

"Before you grasped the implications of what you were doing, because you were still intent on your plan, you turned Julio's body back around to the original facing position. This caused his head to fall forward on the desk and his blood to drip over the blotter. Too late you realized that you'd now made it appear — because of the turnaround, and where the blood was dripping, and so on — as if Julio's killer were right-handed. You couldn't swivel the body back, because the presence and location of the blood-stains on the desk would give away the fact that the body had been turned after the blow. What could you do to reinstate your left-handedness clue? You solved the problem by leaving Julio's body as it then was — that is, head resting forward on the desk — but moving both the desk and the swivel chair-cum-body from its original cater-cornered position to the position from which a left-handed blow could have been delivered."

"That's all pretty devious," the murderer said, smiling again.

"You've a devious mind," Ellery said. "Very much like mine, in fact. Oh, another feature of your frame-up of Marco: those signs of a struggle you left for us. There'd been, of course, no struggle at all, as Marco truthfully assured us. But you had to dress your set in such a way as to justify the overturning of the ashtray in order to plant the shoeprint clue, and an apparent struggle between Julio and Marco provided the obvious justification. You knew of the bad feeling then existing between Nino's two brothers because of Julio's failure to agree on the Canadian oil-lands proposal, and from bad feeling to hand-to-hand combat appeared to you — as you were confident it would appear to the police — a logical next step.

"The truth is," Ellery went on, stretching his long legs so far that his shoe tips almost touched the murderer's, "the truth is your frame-up of

Marco was by far the clumsiest thing you've done. Well, it was your maiden crime. But even in your clumsiness you were lucky. Marco was the weak sister — so to speak — of the brothers; he wasn't strong or stable enough to stand up under the pressures you thoughtfully exerted, especially when he was so drunk. So he did a better job of it than you did: he obligingly hanged himself, giving the police the perfect straw to grasp: that Marco killed Julio and committed suicide in drunken remorse. This was precisely what you wanted the police to think in the first place.

"As for how you got into 99 East for the murder of Julio without being reported," Ellery continued in the same amiable way, "I can only conjecture. But with your peculiar relationship to the principals, I imagine you had pretty much the run of the premises, so that your comings and goings would hardly be noticed. In any event, before you murdered Julio no crimes had been committed at 99 East, so there was no particular reason for anyone to keep a sharp eye out. Apparently you weren't seen either on your way in or your way out; you managed to slip by the guard.

"To get into 99 East for the Nino Importuna murder you had a different problem. The building had been the scene of a murder and suicide by that time; everyone was security conscious. It's possible, of course, that in spite of that you managed to get by the guard unseen, but I'm inclined to think there's a handier explanation, in which your lucky star played a prominent role. Earlier that evening — how odd! it was 9 o'clock or thereabouts — Virginia had lowered the ladder from the penthouse roof to the roof of the adjoining apartment house one story below in order to slip out for a rendezvous with Peter Ennis. She necessarily left the ladder in the lowered position for her return. You knew nothing about her tryst with Peter; what you were after was a way to get past Gallegher up into the penthouse without being spotted. So you did the logical thing and made for the roof of the adjoining building, too, This was, of course, hours after Virginia had left; just before midnight. To your surprise, there was the ladder, ready to be climbed; whatever device you had brought along to scale that one-story difference now wasn't needed. You climbed the ladder, murdered Nino, and used the same route for your escape, which took place long before the 3:30 A.M. of Virginia's return from Connecticut. You wouldn't have thought it such good luck, I'm afraid, if you'd had any inkling that Virginia had used that ladder earlier in the evening to go off with Peter, as I'll demonstrate in a moment."

The murderer was very sober now.

"Access to the two Importunato apartments and the Importuna penthouse apartment was almost certainly attained by the use of duplicate keys; your affiliation with the principals made it easy for you to procure them. I postulate duplicate keys rather than an inside confederate because you're far too smart an operator to place yourself in some underling's power to blackmail you later, especially with such munificence at stake."

"No wonder you've made your living as a detective-story writer," the murderer remarked. "You have an imagination that's not only agile but double-jointed."

"Thanks for bringing me to the essential point," Ellery said graciously. "You've just confirmed a conclusion I reached before I set up this meeting: You're an A student of character, and you took a graduate course in mine. Now come, you can admit that, can't you?"

"As a matter of principle," the murderer murmured, "I admit nothing. Except that this performance of yours is better than anything playing Broadway, Queen, and it's a lot cheaper."

"The ultimate price to you," Ellery retorted, "will make the scalpers look like philanthropists. At least I hope so.

"But to get back to your study of my character: The minute you found out that I was taking a hand in Julio's murder — you weren't on the scene when I was, but you did keep pumping poor old Peter, didn't you? — you decided that you had to get to know me inside and out. You read my books, I don't doubt; studied some typical cases I'd worked on. You came to the conclusion, correctly, that I'm lured like a fish by the colorful as opposed to the drab and routine; that I'm drawn to the subtle rather than the straight-forward; that by temperament I lean toward the complicated in preference to the simple; in the language of the vulgate, I'm a pushover for the fancy suff. So . . . you plotted your course to go through a complex maze, knowing I'd follow it nose down with a whoop and a holler, and that I'd arrive ultimately at the prize you'd planted for me.

"You took the obligatory-9-months-until-inheritance clue and deliberately tied it in to Nino Importuna's 9-superstition. You've been responsible for obfuscating everything with those illusory 9s. And that was 'a fearful sin,' as Father Brown called it. You know Father Brown? My favorite clergyman of fact or fiction. 'Where does a wise man hide a leaf?' he wants to know. And he answers himself: 'In the forest. But what does he do when there is no forest? . . . He grows a forest to hide it in. A fearful sin.' And that's what you did. You grew a forest.

"You sent Inspector Queen those anonymous messages. Your purpose, however, was different from the one I ascribed to Peter Ennis. What you were really after was to bamboozle *me*. You knew that if you showered me with all those lovely, fantastic 9-clues, sooner or later I'd come up with the leaf-in-the-forest, or pebble-on-the-beach, theory. I can't say I didn't dance dutifully to your tune! I was truly the puppet in the hands of the puppet master. When I'd eliminated every last sham 9, as you planned I should, and still hadn't by my own efforts learned about Peter's lunch with Virginia on December 9, 1966, you made sure the information came into my possession. You sent the 10th and last anonymous message to my father, through him tipping me off.

"This," Ellery went on in his even-tempered drawl, "led to the genuine 9-clue you'd programmed me to base my solution on. I was to expound the theory that Peter Ennis, as the murderer, wanted above all to hide the 9-month gestation period from me, and that to accomplish this end he'd bombarded me with 9s . . . so many 9s that I'd be completely confused and baffled and helpless to reach a solution. This was to be my conclusion about Peter's thinking.

"But your ultimate purpose was even subtler than that. You took the leaf-in-the-forest concept one step further. You not only concealed the crucial leaf, you used the very fact of its concealment to provide me with the wrong answer to the problem. *You maneuvered me into eliminating all the 9s but one, so that on the basis of that remaining one I'd come up at long last with the patsy murderer you'd planned for me to choose from the start.*"

And now they were locked eye to eye, and there was no longer any amusement on the murderer's face, only an advanced alertness, the immobility of an animal at the approach of danger.

"The trouble was," Ellery said in a stripped, clean way, "you grew too big a forest. The last anonymous message did more than you meant it to. It gave me your sham setup solution, yes; but unhappily for you it didn't stop there, as it was supposed to. You didn't know, as I remarked a few minutes ago, that Peter and Virginia had inadvertently provided themselves with an unbreakable alibi for the time of Nino's murder. That their alibi forced me to face the falsity of the solution you'd led me to. Forced me, from the very logic of that fact, to go to *you*.

"Because," Ellery said, and his pace was swifter now, "if Peter — not to mention Virginia — was innocent, as his alibi incontestably proved, then the murderer not only had to be someone else, but someone who possessed the same two qualifications: One, the murderer had to know that Virginia and Peter met for lunch on December 9, 1966; two, he had to satisfy *cui bono,* in the same sense that Peter would have satisfied it by marrying Virginia.

"First qualification: How did the murderer know about that lunch? The answer was embedded like a pearl in Virginia's diary account, toward the end. She had noticed you come into the restaurant; she was afraid that if you spotted her with Peter you'd guess their relationship, and she got Peter to hustle her out through the kitchen. A beautiful fit, isn't it? *Because if Virginia and Peter could have seen you, by exactly the same token you could have seen them.*

And see them you did, otherwise the 10th anonymous message could not have been sent.

"Second qualification: Who benefits? Could you? You certainly could, in the same way Peter would benefit: *through Virginia*. And you were the only other person in the world in that enviable position. What's more, if anything were to interfere with your control of Virginia's half billion dollars — if Peter, say, were to prove an obstacle, or Virginia herself — I'm quite certain you'd be prepared to get rid of either or both. In fact, that may have been your ultimate plan, since the deaths of Virginia and Peter — assuming their marriage — would give you in your own right, as Virginia's only surviving relative, the entire Importuna fortune.

"And then what an orgy of gambling and women and power would be yours at the snap of a finger! Who knows what schemes you've blueprinted for the further glory of yourself, the despised object of Nino Importuna's contempt and charity? Was it to become the Monte Cristo of the 20th century?"

And Ellery uncoiled his length and got to his feet and looked down into the handsome saddle-leather face of Virginia's father.

"Well, was it?" Ellery repeated.

"Something like that," said Wallace Ryerson Whyte.

We hope you have enjoyed this Large Print book. Other G.K. Hall & Co. or Chivers Press Large Print books are available at your library or directly from the publishers.

For more information about current and up-coming titles, please call or write, without obligation, to:

G.K. Hall & Co.
295 Kennedy Memorial Drive
Waterville, ME 04901

Tel. (800) 223-1244
Tel. (800) 223-6121

OR

Chivers Press Limited
Windsor Bridge Road
Bath BA2 3AX
England
Tel. (0225) 335336

All our Large Print titles are designed for easy reading, and all our books are made to last.